THERE IS
A SEASON

Phyllis Houseman

A KISMET™ Romance

METEOR PUBLISHING CORPORATION
Bensalem, Pennsylvania

KISMET™ is a trademark of Meteor Publishing Corporation

To my husband, Jack—writing teacher and best friend. I paid my dues with this one, but it was your gift of time and talent and love that really made it possible.

PHYLLIS HOUSEMAN

The hero and heroine in the books Phyllis writes tend to fall in love very quickly, just as she did with her husband, Jack, when they were eight years old. Unfortunately, Fate then kept them apart for years. During that time, Phyllis studied biology, was a Peace Corps Volunteer in Ecuador, and taught high school in Detroit, Michigan. But when she finally met Jack again, they became engaged on their third date. After marrying and having a daughter and son, they moved to California where they now live northeast of San Francisco.

Other books by Phyllis Houseman:

ONE

"Come on now, you great big soggy things, hold back a bit. Just give me a few more seconds of sunshine and then you can have the sky for the rest of the afternoon."

But the wind-powered clouds completely ignored Beth Cristie's hopeful bargaining and continued playing peekaboo with the sun. As the sky darkened once again, the petite ecologist bit back a string of potent words. Defeated for the moment, she let her camera dangle on its neck strap.

Casting a baleful eye at the speeding clouds, she had to remind herself that the white fleece and gray thunderheads were normal for spring in southwestern Washington State. They belonged. It was she and the others in the documentary crew who were the real intruders.

In fact, looking up at the breach in the volcano's cone, Beth thought that the ruined northern slopes of Mount St. Helens resembled a lifeless lunar landscape.

It had been more than a dozen years since the huge eruption that had destroyed the volcano's picture-perfect shape. But from this angle the event might have occurred yesterday, and Beth knew that another eruption could happen again at any time.

A century from now—or today. Nobody really knew.

Ignoring the shudder that went through her body, she pushed up her protective goggles to her forehead in order to get a better view of the thin plume rising from the lava dome. Smelling the sulfur in the air, she recalled the radio communiqué Ruth had received this morning, putting them on alert.

The scientists from the U.S. Geological Survey had monitored new signs of activity on the mountain. Ash and steam displays had cracked the thin crust capping the lava dome. From her position on the edge of the Pumice Plain, Beth couldn't actually see into the caldera, but she could visualize what was happening inside.

Most of the experts thought that the mountain was just rumbling and stretching like a sleepy bear before settling down for another centuries-long hibernation. Still, the authorities were concerned enough to take precautions, as if a new eruptive phase might begin. A warning had gone out yesterday clearing hikers and climbers off the slopes. The Forest Service and National Monument employees also asked tourists to leave the trails surrounding the volcano.

The call this morning had advised people with study permits—like field scientists and Beth's documentary crew—to be on the alert and ready to move out on short notice. To their relief, the group was told that they would probably be able to complete their week-long schedule.

Nevertheless, Beth had felt the sudden need to go into high gear, to speed up the completion of her part of the assignment. That's why she was so desperate to finish taking these pictures. She wanted to show the courageous battle nature was waging in repopulating a disaster zone. In the few days she had been on Mount St. Helens, she had found many examples to confirm the resiliency of life.

After glancing at the clouds again, she refocused her attention on the celery-green bracken fern she had discovered clinging bravely to a shallow crevice in a large boulder. Color slides of the tenacious plant would help remind everyone that nature could come back under the most severe conditions.

If only she could get her camera and the light synchronized.

It was maddening, morning snow had turned to drizzle at noon. Now the rain had finally ended, but sun and cloud fought for dominance. Every time Beth tried to take a picture, she had to reset her ancient Nikon.

However, she was determined to get this shot. She quickly checked the light meter, and before the reading could change, she snapped the shutter.

"All right!" she shouted in triumph, and then tempted the fates by going for a close-up shot. Rapidly changing lenses, she bent over the tiny plant. Just as she activated the button, a flurry of stinging particles hit her cheeks and forehead.

She instinctively closed her lids to protect her eyes from the scratchy material. When she dared open them again, Beth laughed out loud, seeing that the ash was being kicked up by a scurrying pocket gopher. It was frantically tunneling through the windswept cinders that threatened to cover the entrance to its burrow.

Still grinning, she waited for the perfect pose so that she could add the gopher to her pictorial study. Beth felt elated at finding the little creature.

"You hang in there, kids." She gave the fern and gopher a whimsical word of encouragement. "It takes more than a little ash to get rid of us flora and fauna, right?"

The words had hardly been whipped out of her mouth by the persistent wind when the gopher literally disappeared. Muttering in exasperation, Beth gave in to a deep-seated habit and pushed up the sleeves of her thick wool sweater above her elbows.

She intently surveyed the ten-foot-high jumble of boulders and debris that had collected against the mountain's lower slope, searching the tiny animal's territory. With eyes watching the rocks for any movement, she ran around the piles of stone, hoping to catch the rodent popping out of a side tunnel.

Unexpectedly, when she rushed to the far side of the massed rubble, instead of finding the elusive animal, she slammed into a delicate-looking array of scientific equipment attached to a tripod.

Whenever she thought about it later, Beth always remembered the scene as a slow-motion sequence of expanded time and languid movement. In reality, she instantly launched herself into a gravity-defying arabesque, desperately reaching for the instrument package before it could fall.

As her hands closed around the device, Beth was thrown off balance. She managed to roll when she hit the ground, but her uncovered elbows still took the force of the fall.

Gritting her teeth against the sting of scraped skin, she tried to get to her feet. She had just gotten to her knees when a shadow swooped down on her. The salvaged mechanism was wrested from her hands, and she found herself staring up into a set of mirrored goggles.

"You klutz! You almost ruined ten thousand dollars worth of irreplaceable seismic equipment. Not to mention wasting the six hours it took me to set up the experiment. Come on, get off the ground. I'm going to report you to the Forest Service. I'd run you the hell off this mountain myself, but it's their job to deal with brainless kids who ignore their warnings."

Beth glared up at the tall man, obstinately defying his order to get off her knees. *What an ingrate*, she thought.

All he cared about was his equipment, he hadn't even noticed her injured elbows!

"What do you mean, *you're* going to report me?" she shouted up at him. "This is all your fault. Only a fool would stick that damned junk where anybody could run into it. Go ahead, call the Forest Service office, I can't wait for them to get here. They'll be glad to verify my credentials and probably ticket you for reckless endangerment."

When the man colorfully muttered his disbelief, Beth's large amber eyes widened. But she wasn't going to let him intimidate her with his language or by the way his huge body leaned over her.

"Hey, where did you get those funny goggles?" she gibed. "I bet it was from the same person who sold you your certification into the restricted area . . . Bozo the Clown!"

Beth knew that her challenge might have lost a little of its power, because her voice had been reduced to a husky whisper by the ash and sulfur in the air. However, his reaction was still gratifying.

"Clown? Clown!" he shouted. The man whipped off the protective lenses. The exact color of his eyes eluded her in the glaring sunlight, but somehow it added to the fury blazing from them.

The force of his stare hit Beth right where she had always thought her soul was located—exactly between the eyes. Even in the midst of her outrage, she found herself reacting to his masculine strength and ruggedly handsome face. While he went off again, ranting about her failings, she fought the tug of an attraction that was all the more compelling because she had never felt anything like it before.

Shaking her head in a concerted effort to rid herself of the unwanted emotion, Beth's short hair reframed her face in a sun-tipped halo of light-brown curls.

My God, look at that! Joshua Hunter's tirade dried up in midsentence when his eyes were captured by the golden nimbus surrounding the girl's head. Long seconds passed before he could pull his attention away from the glorious sight, to really examine her face and body for the first time.

In his fury at having his experiment upset, he had thought that a thoughtless teenager had blundered into camp. Now he realized that though she was small and slight, her bulky sweater hid the shape of a grown woman. Feeling an instantaneous wave of guilt when he found himself staring at the high rise of her breasts, Joshua's eyes snapped back to her face. The delicate features were nearly as enticing, and he almost groaned out loud. In desperation, he narrowed his eyes to slits, fighting to regain his initial rage.

Beth felt a blush threatening her cheeks while the man completed his sweep of her body and then looked into her face once again. *Now* was the time to get up off the ground and split, she decided. She'd go find Ruth and head back to camp to prepare for dinner. Rearranging the strap of her camera on her neck, she awkwardly struggled to get on her feet.

The man instantly shifted the equipment he was still holding to his left hand and held out the right one to help her. Beth hit it away. She immediately regretted the violent gesture; her elbows stung so much that she gasped in pain. Yet, somehow the agony was easier to bear than the hot discomfort his scrutiny had caused her.

The sound of her pain was hidden by the scrape of feet on loose rock behind her. Beth whirled around, expecting to see her coproducer, Ruth Murray. But a man, an older, more weather-beaten version of the angry giant next to her, was striding over from a large tent she hadn't noticed until that moment.

"What's going on out here, Josh? From the sound of

it, I thought we were having another earthquake." He paused, looking down at Beth. "Now I find that it was you, yelling at this pretty little bit of a girl."

His nonthreatening inspection of Beth's features caused none of the confusion the younger man's appraisal had given her. But not in any mood to respond to his flattery, she just peered warily up at him.

"My God! Look at her poor elbows."

His perceptive blue eyes must have seen the way she was carefully holding her damaged arms, Beth realized.

"Those are nasty scrapes you've got there, miss. How in the world did this happen? Oh . . ." His gaze had gone to the jumble of metal on the ground. The collapsed tripod told most of the story.

"Joshua Jeremiah Hunter, why are you just standing there? Put down that infernal thing-a-ma-bob and get some soap and water for this wounded lady. Let's get her cleaned up and bandaged," he directed in a drawl Beth belatedly recognized as Texan.

The man called Joshua had the grace to look abashed when he finally noticed that Beth had hurt herself. His eyes caught hers for an instant of apology. It seemed to Beth that his attention wandered her face for a measurable beat of time. Then he sent up a muffled curse and turned on his heel. In a dozen long strides, he had reached the tent and disappeared inside.

With his overwhelming presence gone, Beth looked around for the first time, finding that the shelter was only part of an elaborate field-laboratory setup. The clearing was dotted with expensive-looking scientific equipment. Picturing the makeshift camp she shared with the others in her documentary crew, she felt a momentary twinge of jealousy.

"I'm Stuart Hunter, miss. That rude young fellow in there is my son, Joshua. I don't understand why he's acting so contrary, I know I taught him better manners."

Even in the midst of her pain and anger, Beth felt like laughing out loud. The "young" man his father referred to must be in his midthirties. And he sure didn't look like the type who would happily accept the dressing down he had just received from anyone, even his father.

It was as much the prospect of seeing the son get his just desserts as the deep, soothing sound of Stuart Hunter's voice that overcame Beth's reluctance to go into the tent. Inside, Joshua had already set out a complete first-aid kit, along with soap and water.

But when he reached out to help her, Beth's voice vibrated harshly in a low whisper. "No, don't touch me. Keep your hands off my elbows. I'll clean them myself."

"Now, why don't you let him do it? My son's a doctor." A devilish grin creased the father's face. "A doctor of geology, I'll admit, but at one time, he really was a fine paramedic. He's dealt with a lot worse than those scrapes. Right, Josh?"

Throwing his father a quick nod, *Dr*. Hunter then captured Beth around the waist and sat her down on a chair next to the field table.

"Oh! What do you think you're doing?" she sputtered.

"You are going to stay there. The scrapes have got to be cleaned right away before infection sets in. Sit still and it won't hurt, move around, and it will. It's up to you. Either way, I'm going to treat those wounds."

Beth was distracted from her protest by the irrelevant fact that Joshua's deep, authoritative voice lacked his father's broad Texas accent. He began working on her right elbow, carefully wiping liquid soap on it before she knew what was happening.

"Hey, would you watch what you're doing," she said weakly in a final token protest. His fingers automatically tightened on her wrist to prevent her from pulling away. She was very aware of the strength in the huge hand that firmly gripped her. He could have snapped the bone's small circumference with a negligent twist of long sun-tanned fingers.

"Do you also have a degree in torture?" she complained when he directed a stinging stream of water over the wound. The sarcasm helped dampen the unsettling effect his touch was having on her.

"Now, don't start crying like a baby," he taunted in return, evidently angered by her reaction to his careful work.

Beth clamped down tightly on the automatic burning tears that popped into the corners of her eyes at his words, willing them not to fall.

"Great bedside manner," she muttered. "The medical world is still reeling from its loss to geology."

Joshua chuckled, but just began to wash her other elbow. Beth stoically endured the rest of the process until he finally patted the area dry with sterile gauze. Taking hold of her wrist once more, he bent his dark head close to Beth's while he examined the wound on her right elbow. Only inches separated her lips from the thick, long hair which fell over his forehead on to deep furrows of concentration.

His preoccupation allowed Beth to make a covert scan of his face. Her eyes slid past the beautiful black lashes that brushed his lean cheeks. Her gaze skimmed the straight perfection of his nose, and not daring to linger on a finely molded, sensuous mouth, Beth's attention was snared by a strong, regular pulsation that beat under his harshly etched jawline.

As she watched that steady throb, it seemed to quicken in tempo until Beth was sure its rate had doubled. With his increased pulse, she became conscious that the faint, clean male scent surrounding him had thickened to the unmistakable lure of masculine arousal.

The fingers still grasping her wrist had closed so tightly that the pressure now pained more than her torn skin.

When he applied the sudden, cold sting of an antiseptic spray that first agonized and then numbed the region with blessed relief, Beth allowed a whispered protest to escape her lips.

"It really hurts."

"I know. I'm sorry. It'll stop in a second," his deep voice murmured.

"No . . . not the spray. I mean the way you're squeezing my wrist."

The force was instantly removed and a flush ran rampant over his high cheekbones. Without another word, Joshua applied large dressings to the wounds, finishing his work with neat, secure taping.

"Leave those on till tonight and try to keep out of the ash. Let the wounds air-dry while you're sleeping, then cover them during the day until they're healed."

The cold professionalism in his voice made Beth wonder if she had misinterpreted the whole episode. Then he scanned her upturned face, his gaze lingering long seconds on her mouth. Unconsciously, his tongue moistened his own lower lip. Beth held her breath. Waiting . . . waiting . . . until a shudder went through the man's wide shoulders and he abruptly turned away to clean up the used materials.

The chair, the tent, the older man tactfully paging through a heavy book, all became part of Beth's universe again.

From the bunk where he was repacking the metal first-aid box, the tall geologist cleared his throat. Begrudgingly, like the words hurt, she heard him grumble.

"Don't worry about the equipment. You didn't break anything. I'll just have to spend the rest of the day recalibrating the settings."

How gracious! Perhaps because she was so shaken, Beth had an almost irresistible urge to stick out her tongue at the broad back as the man deftly stowed the bandages and antiseptic into their box.

She was prevented from completing that gratifying gesture by a familiar "Yoo-hoo." Ruth Murray stuck her red-haired head into the tent.

For Beth, the deep-green eyes and freckles on Ruth's face always conjured up an Irish lilt to her friend's voice, even though her family had come over a hundred years earlier.

"I found your notebook on the ground out there, and I knew you couldn't be far away," her current employer joked. The slight traceries of laugh lines around her eyes were the only hint that the tall woman was over forty.

"My God, it must have fallen out of my pocket!" Beth knocked over the chair, rushing to examine her journal of observations for damage.

"Beth, nothing's lost, for heaven's sakes. But what happened to you? Why are your elbows bandaged?"

"Oh, just a minor accident, and the wounds have been treated by an expert, I'm told." Beth smiled wryly at the two men who had been listening to the exchange between the women. "Losing this record would have been a real disaster. It's worth more than my camera and everything else I own put together."

She waved the notebook at the self-centered son-of-a-Texan. Beth wanted to emphasize to him that her attempt to save his equipment had endangered her own irreplaceable property.

The man opened his mouth to say something, but Stuart Hunter interrupted his son. "Is everything there?"

When Beth nodded, he smiled his relief. Then he turned toward Ruth, blue eyes glittering in the maturely handsome face.

"Ma'am, I'm Stuart Hunter, and this is my son, Joshua." He indicated the younger man with a nod of his head. Joshua acknowledged Ruth with a half smile and a handshake.

So he did know the social graces when he wanted to, Beth realized with a defiant lift of her chin. A biting comment formed on her lips, but Stuart had begun explaining recent events to Ruth in more detail.

"Your little friend had an altercation with Josh's laser experiment. We've got her patched up and there's no real damage to the apparatus. But you know, I'd like to make it up to her—to both of you—for the inconvenience. Would you ladies do us the honor of having a campfire dinner tonight?"

"Oh, no, we couldn't!" Beth declined forcefully.

Ruth's answer was much louder than her own husky protest. "Mr. Hunter, I'm Ruth Murray and this is Beth Cristie. We'd love to come to dinner. However, there are two more people in our party. Phil Price, our motion picture photographer, and Dana Clark, the sound technician. I wouldn't want to strain your resources."

"We've got more than enough for everyone, especially if any of the others is as tiny as this one." He smiled down on Beth, his head twelve inches higher than her five foot two.

Now that was enough of that, Beth thought. "Mr. Hunter, why do you keep going on about my height? My feet touch the ground just like yours, and surely that's all we can ask of them, isn't it? You've heard the old cliché . . ."

". . . good things come in small packages," they finished together.

"Well, Miss Cristie, I didn't mean any offense. I want you to know that I think short women are just fine." Giving Ruth a quick appraisal, he hastily added, "Of course, I like tall women, too."

Beth and Ruth both laughed out loud at his quick recovery. As far as Beth was concerned, that laughter should have signaled a cheerful end to the subject of her height.

Then Joshua Hunter had to add his own comment to the conversation.

Standing at the tent flap, he offered a variation of another old cliché. "Dad, I think a better saying would have been, 'Beware of little klutzes carrying cameras.' "

Before Beth could sputter out a reply to that, Joshua had snatched up his own camera off a bunk and ducked outside. Taking bench-mark pictures so that he could reset the laser device seemed a good excuse to get away from the happy little trio. What in the world was his father thinking of, inviting them to a cookout? He knew that there was work to be done, experiments that literally could make the difference between life and death. And with the volcano heating up . . . Cursing beneath his breath, Joshua stalked to the tripod Beth had knocked over and picked it up.

A few seconds later, Beth came out of the tent behind Ruth and Stuart. She was fuming, but the older people were deep in conversation, making plans for the dinner that night.

Well, eating in the presence of the galling Joshua Hunter was way down on Beth's list of fun activities. She decided to let Ruth know about her feelings on the way back to their own camp, located a half mile north of here, along a carefully marked, ash-strewn path.

Not even aware of what she was doing, Beth's eyes tracked Joshua while he moved around the camp, intent on his picture-taking. *What a marvelous name*, she mused . . . Joshua Jeremiah. The biblical label seemed to fit his larger-than-life physique. His body was the most perfect one she had ever seen, somehow even better than Phil's tall, muscular frame.

Joshua's broad shoulders and chest looked like they belonged to a champion diver, rather than to a muscle builder or football player. His narrow waist and hips were almost one measurement. They blended with a flat stomach and strong, well-shaped thighs that were encased in tight denim jeans.

Beth abruptly squeezed her eyes shut. She couldn't believe she was actually taking such a detailed inventory of this hateful man. Forcefully, she dwelt on the masculine qualities of interest to a mature woman of twenty-nine. She should be looking for a man with a sense of humor, a purpose in life, common goals and interests. Someone like Phillip Price.

No, not like Phil. Beth had known the motion-picture photographer for six months. After going out with him a few times, she had found that each date had been less fun than the last. And since they had arrived on the mountain, he had been acting even stranger. She had been meaning to say something about his behavior to Ruth.

Beth found herself looking at Joshua again and absently computing the ratio of the man's shoulder-to-hip measurements. Pretty damned perfect.

Oh, God! *Move eyes*, she demanded of her optic muscles. *Check out the status of the volcano. Count dead pine trees. Anything, but don't keep looking at that man.* However, Beth Cristie found it impossible to tear her gaze away from Joshua Hunter.

She watched him take one last picture and then begin reattaching the device to the tripod. A satisfied smile lit her face when she noticed that Joshua placed it well away from the spot where she had fallen.

Her attention was finally wrested away from the man when Ruth came over, with Stuart Hunter trailing close behind.

"If you're finished for the day, Beth, let's go back to our camp and collect Phil and Dana."

"Just what kind of work are you doing here, ladies?" Stuart asked.

"Well, I've got a grant from the Public Broadcasting System to make a short documentary on the reestablishment of life on Mount St. Helens,'' Ruth explained, waving the clipboard she always seemed to be carrying. ''This afternoon, I was out scouting locales, while Beth took some stills to help illustrate the script we're collaborating on. I do the writing and Beth supplies the scientific expertise.''

Somehow, Stuart looked impressed and worried at the same time. ''You know, you shouldn't have separated like that. With this new activity, a lot worse things can happen around here than scraped elbows,'' he admonished sternly, although his voice had dropped to barely a whisper.

''Oh, I was only a few hundred yards up the trail,'' the supremely independent Ruth Murray informed him with surprising mildness.

Beth looked at her boss carefully; she certainly was acting weird.

''So you two work for a television station?'' Stuart probed.

''No, I teach documentary film production at UCLA and Beth's a postdoc ecologist who wandered into one of my classes. She only wanted to learn how to script a nature movie the biology department was making, but we discovered that she also has a native talent for still photography.''

''Are you *still* planning to be a naturalist, Miss Cristie?'' Stuart punned.

Beth didn't try to stifle the required groan. ''I've been a working ecologist for a few years, Mr. Hunter. Besides using material I'm collecting here for our film, I'm on assignment from *Science in America* magazine. I'm their part-time West Coast stringer. The head of the Los Angeles office retires this year, and after I finish up my research project at UCLA, the publication wants me to take over the job.''

Beth immediately felt like clamping her hand over her mouth. She was babbling like an idiot. *Why don't you show him pictures of your three sisters and your parents. And I'm sure he'd be fascinated to learn exactly when you found out there was no Santa Claus,* she scolded herself.

Stuart Hunter didn't seem to mind her gushing. He just said, "Sounds like you've got your life all planned out. What are you researching, Miss Cristie?"

"Oh, please call me Beth. Well, the topic of my doctoral dissertation was, 'Life under Stress: Nature's Prolific Response to the Threat of Extinction.' I did my field research at Yellowstone, during the big fires. I'm planning a follow-up trip there later this year. I'm also finding all sorts of interesting parallels here. Wish I had more time on the volcano to do a rigorous comparison of the two disasters." She sighed.

The expressive lift of Stuart Hunter's eyebrow either acknowledged her scholarship or the ability to recite that mouthful of a title, Beth decided with a grin.

While they were talking, she noticed out of the corner of her eye that Joshua hovered nearby, almost as if he were eavesdropping on the conversation. However, when she looked directly at him, he immediately walked to the other end of the camp where he turned on a portable seismograph. The vibrating needles started to move over the rotating drum, recording the restless mountain's grumblings.

"Just what are *you* doing here?" Beth finally gave in to her own curiosity about the men.

"Oh, we're testing out a little do-hickey for the government. They're interested in an idea Josh and I came up with. We hope it'll give several days' advance warning of dangerous activity around volcanic and earthquake zones," he confided. "I originally messed around with the concept for a company I own, to help us search out deep-lying deposits of crude oil and gas. But Josh has really done most of the work. He's spent thousands of hours refining a prediction formula over the last several years, even while he's been teaching full-time at the University of Texas."

Beth looked at the seamed face carefully, and for the first time saw that behind Stuart Hunter's "good-ol'-boy" facade dwelt the mind of an intelligent, highly trained scientist.

"We were just going to take some important readings when you fell into our laps, Beth. So don't be too hard on Joshua. I know he's on a short fuse. God knows, that's understandable given the circumstances," he mumbled to a finish.

Beth felt an uneasy twinge of disquiet sweep over her. She had no idea of its source. Just that something was very wrong here. High-voltage tension flowed around this camp, between father and son, with its point of origin being Joshua Hunter. Mentally shaking herself, she decided that whatever the problem, it was none of her concern. She would never see him—them—again.

"Anyway," Stuart was saying, "we'll be looking forward to the cookout tonight. How about five or so? You know how cold it gets here, so an early supper is the best way to go."

"You're on, Mr. Hunter," Ruth answered for the both of them before Beth could decline again.

"That's Stuart to you, honey. We Texans don't stand on much formality, Ruth."

"Sure, Stu, *sweetie*," she countered, "us Californians can beat you at informality any day." Ruth laughed and then started when a minor temblor ran under their feet.

Stuart Hunter threw a quick look over to his son, who was glaring at him. As the younger man stalked over, his father said hurriedly, "Well, see you at dinner."

"OK," Ruth agreed. "We'll bring along the best that Public Television can provide . . . Beans."

When the two women walked away from the camp, a pair of narrowed eyes watched them until they disappeared. In the cool mountain air, a line of sweat beaded Joshua's long upper lip.

Danger, he thought. *Sweet and beautiful danger. Maybe I can use the cookout tonight to convince her to leave the mountain as quickly as possible.*

He'd have to be careful doing it, though. He couldn't look at her too much. He shouldn't get near enough to breathe in her scent, which somehow neutralized the pungent bite of sulfur in the air. But most of all, he didn't dare touch her again.

TWO

Beth argued with Ruth the entire way back to their camp.

"How could you accept for us like that, Ruth? *I* never want to set eyes on the jackass again. Oh, he got me so angry. All he cared about was that damned setup. He didn't even notice my elbows until his father got on his case."

"Honey, you've got to admit he's also the second most gorgeous creature you've ever laid your eyes on." Ruth laughed.

"Who's the first—the elder Mr. Hunter?" Beth scoffed.

"You bet his size thirteen Texan boots he is," she confirmed.

"I'm surprised at you. I thought Harry cured you of men."

"All Harry cured me of was marriage. In the seven years since the divorce, I've dated a lot of guys, but I haven't seen one I'd even consider trying to put up with again, until . . ." She paused thoughtfully.

"Until today? Ruth, what's gotten into you? You're

really acting strange. What about his wife? One usually goes along with a son, you know."

"Oh, Stu's a widower." She smiled wickedly.

Beth stopped walking to stare at her grinning friend with reluctant admiration.

"How ever did you find that out? You didn't talk to the man alone for more than two minutes!"

"Well, I always make sure I know what's what. Now, your fellow, Josh, may be another matter. That man's all tied up, somehow." She pondered for a moment. "I haven't figured it out just yet. But I will by tonight," she confidently predicted.

"What do you mean, *my* fellow? You've conveniently forgotten that I've been going out with Phil. I'm not the least bit interested in your 'second most gorgeous male.' I'm surprised at you, to be taken in by a pretty face. All Joshua Hunter impressed me with was his rudeness! Besides, don't you think that Phil could match him in a handsomeness contest?"

Beth wasn't sure why she was defending a man she had dated so casually. She had been ready to talk to Ruth about the frightening possessiveness Phil had revealed recently, and here she was playing devil's advocate for him. Her contrariness must be because of the infuriating Joshua Hunter and Ruth's matchmaking attempt.

"Oh, come on, Beth. How often have you gone out with Phil—half a dozen times? What do you really know about the man? I'll grant you that he's handsome and can be very charming, but don't tell me that you're serious about him. I've watched the two of you together. Whatever he's feeling, you don't share it. He's just not right for you. In fact, since we hiked up here, I've been wondering if he's just not right, period. He's been forgetful and moody and reluctant to do some of his work."

Trust Ruth to get to the heart of the matter. However, Beth stubbornly continued her defense.

"Ruth, Phillip is one of the best motion-picture nature photographers in the business. And he's been so considerate and well mannered with me. Not like some others I could name," she muttered. "In fact, this morning, Phil asked me to . . . to . . . well, go steady—if anyone older than sixteen still uses that term. I'm thinking about it, I really am. I'll probably be able to give him an answer after this trip."

Beth was all too aware of waffling. Talk about wishy-washy! Ruth smiled a little grin that said she heard the doubt in Beth's voice. Somehow, Beth couldn't be angry with her friend, the blatant relief on that freckled face was too obvious.

"Well, we'll talk about it some more when you get over being mulish," the older woman said. "I do apologize for pushing Joshua Hunter at you, though. And I'm not really worried that you'll run into Phil's arms just to spite me or that great big beautiful Texan."

Beth found herself laughing out loud. She gave Ruth a quick hug and they resumed walking toward camp with more energy in their step. No, she wasn't about to ruin her life by jumping into an ill-considered relationship with Phil. Somehow, he had begun to frighten her even more than the tremors that had rumbled under their feet in the last two days and the ash that had vented from the volcano this afternoon.

Hiking along, Beth silently rehearsed how best to sever her tenuous relationship with the man.

Fifteen minutes later, the two women arrived at their camp. In the middle of the clearing, Phillip Price and Dana Clark, the sound technician, were working over some videotape footage they had taken earlier in the day. Phil looked up from where his head had been bent in concentration, close to that of the flaxen-haired girl. He smiled brightly at Beth.

Beth had to admit that everything about Phil was bright:

his beachboy-blond hair; his perfect teeth; the light-blue eyes; and his quick intelligence.

So why did she feel like grimacing when he blew her a kiss, before returning to the preview machine he had been cranking? After shedding her equipment, she plopped down against the gaunt gray trunk of a scorched pine tree. Coughing within the sulfurous little hurricane of ash she had raised, Beth closed her eyes. Her lids became a mini-movie screen for the memory of her first meeting with the cameraman last semester.

They had been sharing a table in the university's crowded library. She had been attracted to Phil's gleaming white smile when he leaned over to introduce himself. Yet what really impressed her was his offer to quiz her on the scientific names of the hundred North American birds she was trying to learn for her final exam in an ornithology class.

An hour later, Beth was confident that the elusive birds wouldn't fly from her brain again. She offered to buy coffee for Phil, as payment for his services.

After acing the test, Phil took her out to dinner in celebration. They seemed to have everything in common, from a deep concern for the world's ecology to a love of photography. She had such a good time that in the next few months, Beth went out with him whenever she had a free moment. It was not nearly as often as Phil would have liked.

His intense interest was flattering. What woman wouldn't want to be pursued by such a generous, talented, and good-looking man? She even encouraged him to apply to Ruth for a position on the Mount St. Helens' expedition, and Beth was very happy when he got the job.

Soon after, however, her feelings began to change. Just before the trip, they had gone to a faculty tea together. It was at the function last week that Beth finally acknowledged a disturbing pattern in Phil's behavior.

She had smiled a greeting to an old flame at the get-together and chatted with him for a few minutes. Phil glowered at her all the time she talked to the man or to any other male at the gathering. On the way home he cautioned her to be careful, telling Beth that her smile produced a devastating effect on strong men's knees.

Thinking that he was kidding, she had joked, "Well, Phil, if I ever run out of money, I can always patent my lips and sell my teeth to the Army."

"Very funny, darling. But you've missed the point; your smile is *mine*." He had reached over to stroke her cheek. Beth barely kept from shuddering as he went on talking. "I don't want you squandering it on any other man."

"Shades of 'My Last Duchess,' " Beth muttered to herself, recalling Robert Browning's wicked little poem. Then, remembering the few dates they had gone on, she realized that Phil had become a little more possessive each time she was with him. During those dates, she had also found that he sometimes hid a strange moodiness behind his brilliant smile.

It might have been because of Vietnam. He had told her on their second night out that he had been there. Listening to Phil's stories on the subject, one might think that his years in that war-ravished country had been a lark. Yet when she asked a couple of questions that went beneath the surface of the tales, he had clammed up. Beth hadn't pushed; she understood that many men didn't want to talk about the war. Besides, she didn't have any right to probe. After all, theirs was just a casual friendship.

Phil had tried to change that this morning. He had stopped her after breakfast, just as Beth had been going toward her tent to gather up her equipment for the day's work. Getting her alone, he announced that he wanted to deepen their relationship. He wanted them to see each other exclusively.

Confused, Beth had pleaded the press of work and put him off. But now, as she returned from her reverie, she knew that she had come to a decision. She just wasn't interested in pursuing a romantic relationship with Phillip Price.

But how to tell him? With growing agitation, Beth pushed up on her sweater sleeves and gasped when her hands ran over the bandages firmly attached to her torn skin. The disturbing attraction she had instantly felt for Joshua Hunter surfaced again, adding to her quandary.

Yet those feelings reaffirmed that Phil wasn't right for her. Otherwise, how could she have reacted so strongly to a stranger—a hostile, rude stranger at that? It was obviously time to confront Phil.

She jumped up from her tree backrest. Luckily, Phillip had just finished his work. He walked over to Beth and gave her an affectionate hug.

"I missed you today," he said. "Get any good shots?"

"Yes, I think so. A few, anyway. Phil, about what you said this morning . . . we need to talk."

"Great! I was just thinking the same thing. Let's get a bit of privacy. Come on."

As Beth allowed Phil to lead her through a stand of denuded trees, he noticed her bandaged elbows. She told him about her experience with Joshua Hunter and his father. At least she told him the bare essentials.

"Sounds like a real winner, that guy. Why does Ruth want to have dinner with such a pair?"

"Oh, Stuart Hunter is really nice. Maybe the son was a foundling." She laughed. "No, he couldn't be. Looks just like his dad must have, twenty years ago."

Beth firmly put aside the virile picture that had sprung, unbidden, into her brain. "I'll bet they serve something more than hot dogs tonight. You should have seen their camp. Money! I wonder what department of the government is funding them. Perhaps Ruth can apply to it for a project grant. Or maybe the Hunters are independently wealthy. I even saw a site cleared so a helicopter could land right there. They sure didn't backpack all that equipment in, like we did.''

"Well, speaking of future projects, sweetheart," Phil smiled into her eyes, "let's have your answer. No, wait. Forget about what I said this morning. I don't think we should just date each other exclusively. As far as I'm concerned, I have no need for a courtship. Let's get married. When we're done here, we can exchange our plane tickets to L.A. for a trip to Las Vegas. We can be married on Saturday!''

"Married? Saturday! Phil, what in the world are you talking about? We hardly know each other. We may have met six months ago, but we haven't seen each other a half dozen times since then. No one should take such a serious step so quickly. Anyway, I'm in no position to get married. I have to finish my postdoctoral research. I have to start my new job, and . . .''

Beth knew that she was babbling, but she had never been so shocked or surprised in her life.

Phil just laughed at her sputtering. "Don't worry, honey. I know all I need to about you.''

Before she could move away, he pulled her roughly against himself, sweeping her off her feet so that startled amber eyes were level with his own pale blue.

"We don't have to wait," he grated. "You have to say yes." His mouth took hers, his kiss containing a passion he had never expressed before.

With her hands splayed on his shoulders, Beth tried to push away, frightened by this uncharacteristic force. She suddenly realized how chaste their embraces had been up to now. Phil had never been carried away by the few kisses they had shared.

Now his mouth was rough and his touch demanding. Beth could do nothing but endure the onslaught until he lowered her feet to the ground and loosened his embrace a bit, trying to lift her sweater.

She managed to pull her mouth away from his, but one powerful arm still locked her body to his.

"Phil, this is madness. Let me go. I don't want this. You're holding me too tight. My elbows are hurting and I can hardly breathe."

Her husky pleas finally penetrated. He let her go so abruptly that Beth staggered.

"God, I'm sorry, darling," he muttered. "I wouldn't hurt you for the world." The guilt in his eyes kept Beth from following her first impulse to flee back to the camp.

Taking several deep breaths, she willed herself to calm down. There had to be some way to salvage this situation. She didn't want to make an enemy of Phil. Striving for some control, Beth slowly recovered her poise and tried to defuse the emotional atmosphere with a little humor.

"Well, Phillip, I think there's got to be something about this mixture of sulfur and ash we're breathing. Maybe someone should bottle it. They'd probably become instant millionaires."

Something gleamed in Phil's eyes besides amusement and, feeling panicky again, Beth turned toward the camp. "I think we should go back to the others," she said over her shoulder. "They might get worried that we fell into an ash pit."

"No!" It only took Phillip three long strides to catch up to Beth. He hauled her back into his arms, though he seemed to be taking care not to hold her too tightly or touch her wounds. "No, Beth," he repeated softly. "I want to settle this now. We're getting married as soon as we can arrange it. I want everyone to know that you're mine, Beth. I especially need *you* to know it."

His voice became a husky whisper. "Oh, I'm aware that I've been preoccupied and haven't been open enough with you about myself. Well, that's going to be different from now on." He tilted her chin up and kissed her tenderly.

Not knowing how to deal with such gentleness, Beth found that she couldn't pull away. Phil was trembling, obviously trying to hold back the awakening desire that tormented him. Ironically, this controlled passion finally convinced Beth that she would never feel a response to match his.

She should have been touched by his sweetness. It should have pushed her across the line into loving him. Instead, she found that the emotion just wasn't there; the spark would not ignite. Ruth had been right, Phillip was not the man she needed. He was not the one who could break through the barriers that Beth surrounded her heart.

A polite cough broke them out of the embrace. As if Beth's thoughts had conjured her up, Ruth Murray came around the trees that had blocked them from sight of the camp. Phil immediately let Beth go and she moved a step away from him.

"Sorry, didn't mean to interrupt, but we'd better be off. I don't want to walk to the Hunter camp in the dark. Beth, would you help me get some food packed to take along?" Ruth asked over her shoulder, ambling away.

"I'm coming with you," Beth called, quickly falling in behind the woman. She had never been so glad to see anyone.

When Phil caught up a second later, he just walked beside Beth, quiet and obviously lost in thought. Her brain whirled, too. She shook her head back and forth. Six months ago, she had thought that Phil might be the one. He had seemed so very special in so many ways. Yet, something was also very wrong with the tall, blond man. Something dark and rather frightening. Her body shuddered when she thought about the last several minutes.

"Tonight, honey." He suddenly bent to whisper in her ear. "I've decided. We'll tell everybody at the cookout."

For a second, Phil's words made absolutely no sense to Beth. What in the world was he talking about?

"Tonight?" she echoed. "Tonight!" She abruptly understood, but Phil had already lengthened his stride, marching ahead of her and Ruth toward their camp.

THREE

Beth followed in single file behind Phil as he led the way over the ash-blown trail she and Ruth had marked earlier. He illuminated the shadowed path ahead with a strong beam from the large flashlight he carried.

Shaking her head, Beth wondered for the hundredth time why she had let Ruth steamroll her into going to this cookout. She definitely didn't want to spend the evening with the Hunters, no matter how nice the older man was. Also, there was no way she was going to let Phil announce to the others that she had agreed to marry him.

He seemed to have purposely avoided her while the documentary crew got ready to go to the cookout. Somehow she'd get him alone and explain her feelings again before he could embarrass either of them.

Dana Clark cut into Beth's troubled thoughts with a sotto voce "Damn" when she stumbled on a pebble.

"Phil, let's all close up a little so the light doesn't run ahead of our feet," Ruth suggested from the rear.

He slowed down, and the women bunched together behind him in the gathering of dusk. Now walking next to Dana, Beth found herself glancing at the very tall woman.

Unlike Ruth, whose ample curves were only suggested in her well-cut clothes, Dana flaunted her body, with its more than adequate chest and hips.

She usually wore cutoffs and a tight T-shirt, even in the very crisp spring air of Mount St. Helens. This evening, she had given lip service to the night chill by donning skintight jeans and a lumberman's plaid jacket, worn open over her clinging sweater.

Beth looked down at her own cream-colored fisherman's knit and tried to stifle a sigh of regret. Her high, firm breasts didn't raise the heavy wool to any appreciable degree. Then a ridiculous thought made her chuckle. *If you really wore Dana's bra size at your height, shorty, you'd keep falling over on your nose!*

The warm glow of a campfire suddenly softened the glare of the flashlight Phil carried as they rounded the rocky outcrop that had hidden the clearing from Beth's view earlier in the afternoon.

Stuart Hunter was busily stirring a bubbling pot of clam chowder when they approached.

"Hi there, Ruth, Beth, folks," he drawled a greeting.

"Hello, Stu," Ruth replied. "Stuart Hunter, I'd like you to meet Dana Clark and Phillip Price. Here are the beans, like I promised, plus a few other things," she continued after completing the round of introductions. "Say, it looks like you've got more than a wienie roast planned."

After the man added a small amount of sherry to the chowder, he gave them a lesson in gourmet campfire cooking, doing a passable W. C. Fields imitation.

"Everything's out of a can, my friends. Except this wine, which I brought along for medicinal purposes. Doc says it's good for the heart."

"Oh, Stuart, do you have a heart condition?" Ruth's voice had a strange softness to it.

"Hardly a condition, just a little coronary insufficiency

now and then . . . a mild angina. If I don't try to break the four-minute-mile, I can forget about it," he informed her, falling back into his normal accent. "It certainly won't interfere with anything else." He grinned wickedly at Ruth.

Beth's startled laughter joined with the others when she saw that Ruth actually looked flustered for the first time since she had met the woman.

"Anyway, the chowder's made from clams, dehydrated potatoes and onions, powdered milk, and, of course, the wine. The biscuits are fresh sourdough, and there's a steamed fruit pudding with freeze-dried plums and apples in the kettle."

"Well, you certainly don't need our meager offerings. You're a man who can really feed himself," Ruth complimented, having recovered her poise.

"Oh, we bachelors can survive, if we have to. Rather have a woman's help, though. Why don't you fix those beans? They're good protein."

Opening the can and dumping its contents into a pot, Ruth asked casually, "Is your son also a bachelor?"

Stuart was about to answer when Joshua appeared in the circle of light with an armload of wood. While he put it down, the offspring gave his parent a telling look, as if he had heard the question and wanted to convey that the answer was no business of the guests.

Beth suppressed a dismayed groan. She had tried to convince herself that she had only imagined the man's dark attraction, but his arrival in the fire's glow had ignited a similar warmth deep in her body.

Ruth closed the awkward silence with graceful introductions of the rest of her crew to the younger geologist.

While he shook hands with Joshua, Beth stood next to Phil. Joshua gave the two of them a quick appraisal, and then turned to add fuel to the cookfire. Dana attached herself to the man who fed the blaze, hunched down, Asian-style.

"Have you ever been in a place as awful as this side of the volcano, Josh? I was saying to Phil this afternoon that I'll never get the ash out of my hair." She patted its thickness. "I don't even want to think about what it's doing to my skin. . . ."

Joshua answered Dana's chatter with monosyllabic replies, which didn't seem to faze the girl at all. Abruptly realizing that she was listening, Beth pulled her attention away from the two and went to offer her assistance to Ruth and Stuart.

When it was ready, Beth helped pass out the mugs of hot chowder. She warily gave Joshua his, trying not to spill a drop of its brimming contents. During the slow-motion transfer process, his fingers brushed hers and they felt hotter than the bubbling soup. When her hand started to tremble at his touch, the sardonic look he gave her, with one dark eyebrow slightly raised, made Beth want to dump the whole bowl on his lap.

"You're not hurting, are you?" The surprising, soft query rumbled out of that deep chest.

"Hurting?" Beth didn't know what he meant.

"Your elbows," he clarified.

"Oh, my elbows. No, they're all right," she managed to say.

"Good." He lifted the mug to his finely formed lips. Beth watched him take the first sip as if mesmerized. "So's the chowder," he drawled.

The innocuous procedure of tasting the hot liquid suddenly seemed very intimate, very sensual, and Beth realized how foolish she was, standing there watching the man eat his soup!

Before anyone else noticed her adolescent gawking, she made a graceful pirouette and served the rest of the chowder with the elegance of a prima ballerina. When everyone had settled down to eat, Beth looked around for a place to sit. Phil caught her eye and he cheerfully patted the spot next to him.

Reluctantly, she sat down near the motion-picture photographer. Eating her own bowl of chowder, she tried not to glance at Joshua, who was watching her over the rim of his cup.

Joshua looked at the couple across from him. He observed how the blond man—Price—was behaving around Beth. The guy was obviously a goner. Good. There was nothing for him to worry about. She was attached. He'd get through the next couple of hours and then she'd be gone. Gone, as if she hadn't blessed him with a moment of sunshine after he had lived in a total eclipse for so many years.

Being unable to figure out how Joshua's gaze could be mocking and angry at the same time, Beth decided to ignore him and concentrated on her food. Unfortunately, her field of vision somehow kept colliding with the darkened eyes that met hers across the leaping barrier of flame.

When Phil turned toward Beth to ask her something, he intercepted one such exchange. The slight groove between his fair eyebrows deepened as his gaze followed hers.

Quickly trying to defuse the situation when she saw the too-familiar flush of jealousy rise up Phil's neck, Beth deflected his attention by telling him about her encounter with the pocket gopher that afternoon.

She finished by concocting a slightly ribald ending for her little anecdote. "Anyway, I swear that little devil knew exactly what he was doing, luring me away like that. He probably had a love nest in there, and was afraid that my pictures would put him in a compromising position with the wife and kiddies at home."

Just as she had hoped, Phil's tension visibly lessened when her wicked silliness made him laugh with the others at the ridiculous punch line. With her spirits back to their normal, high level, Beth was able to appreciate the delicious, filling dinner. Her friends all knew that she was blessed with a quick-burning metabolism, allowing her to put away meals at which a longshoreman would balk.

Stuart Hunter couldn't have known that, and he watched what she consumed in amazement. "Young lady, do you always eat like that, or are you just healing your elbows?" he finally asked.

Before Beth could reply, Phil answered, "Oh, I run up a terrific Visa bill every time we go out to dinner. Lord knows, we'll probably have to take out a loan to finance our first year's food budget after we're married."

Nobody seemed to hear Beth's agonized gasp.

"Oh, when are you two taking the big step?" Stuart inquired.

"Soon, just as soon as she says yes." Phil put his arm around Beth as he smiled down on her, waiting. An expectant silence lengthened around the fire.

God, this was just what she had been afraid of! Beth had tried to corner Phil, but she hadn't been able to talk to him alone since they had left their camp.

When he saw that she had no intention of responding, the teasing light gradually changed in Phillip's eyes. Instead, Beth found herself lashed by a blast of rage and reproach lasering out of his crystal-blue lenses. Yet, in spite of Phil's growing anger, she couldn't make herself speak. He finally took his arm away from her shoulder.

The whole episode was playing like Beth's worst Freudian nightmare. But instead of walking naked through a crowd of strangers, this was somehow even worse. She had shown her inability to deal with a delicate situation in front of people whose opinion mattered to her.

Into her bête noir Stuart Hunter tried to inject some of the wholesome good manners that were obviously a part of his character.

"What do you people say to some champagne to finish

this magnificent dinner? . . . whoops, I forgot to get the champagne, guess this sherry will have to do."

He poured a little into each person's coffee mug, probably hoping it would help ease the tension that had been generated. While the group sipped the sherry in the heavy silence, their host poked at the fire with a branch until he finally rallied and cleared his throat.

"What better place than around a campfire on a wicked old witch of a volcano for some good old-fashioned ghost stories. Let's have a contest."

Joshua felt a wave of anger and disbelief surge through his body. How could his father suggest such a competition? Didn't he remember that his son had a tale of horror that would win hands down? A story that would generate such stomach-turning disgust that Beth—everyone—would go running from the campfire.

His eyes automatically searched out that lovely little face glowing in the colorful display of resin-fired flames. A wave of emptiness engulfed him as strongly as anything he had experienced in the last dozen years. He knew that he would never taste her sweetness. Never return the passion he sensed was waiting to be fully tapped.

Joshua felt the dark bulk of the ruined mountain loom closer. The sensation of being watched that had been nagging at him so strongly since returning to Mount St. Helens became almost overwhelming.

However, he couldn't tell if the eyes that monitored his movements were sad and loving, or filled with anger.

Maybe his own personal spectre was no longer satisfied that he relived the same nightmare almost every night. He had devoted more than a decade of his life to trying to make up for the wrong he had done to Carol, but maybe that was not enough.

Perhaps he had angered her spirit this afternoon, when he had looked into Beth's huge amber eyes for the first time and felt a sharp stab of awareness in his loins.

Did Carol want him to confess his crimes to this gathering and let Beth find out just what kind of man he was? Had Carol's ghost somehow prompted his father into suggesting this crazy story-telling contest for that purpose?

Lord, what a way for a scientist to be thinking! Joshua shook his head, trying to rid himself of the rising paranoia. Then he glanced over at his father and almost laughed out loud.

Stuart Hunter was not even looking his way! His father was gazing at Ruth Murray with an almost sappy grin on his face. Joshua finally understood that the older man was only trying to catch the interest of the redheaded lady.

"Come on, Ruth, why don't you go first," Stuart challenged her. "Being a filmmaker, you must know a few good horror tales."

"Me? Heavens, no! I just do documentaries. Why, I haven't told a ghost story since I scared my little girls when I was a camp counselor, lo these—*hummpf!*—many years ago. My specialty was the Ërl König, the Elf King. We'd need a terrified six-year-old to play the part of the prince for that one."

Dana Clark suddenly waved her hand in the air, looking like she was in a classroom. "Hey, guys, I don't know if this qualifies as a ghost story or not. But the first day we got here, I heard one of the interpretive guides at the Windy Ridge Lookout telling a group of tourists how Ape Canyon got its name."

She stopped speaking abruptly and then said almost defensively, "I think it was sort of scary." When Stuart gave her an encouraging nod, Dana smiled shyly and cleared her throat before going on.

"Well, it seems that back in 1924, some miners from Longview had a cabin up here, near their work site on the east side of the mountain. The place was next to a deep canyon, south of the Plains of Abraham. Anyway, one evening just before sunset, several huge, hairy animals appeared. They surrounded the cabin and began throwing boulders at it. The men spent the night huddled inside. The next morning, the seven-foot-tall, apelike creatures were still around. The frightened miners shot at them, hitting one. Its body rolled down into the narrow ravine at the beginning of the canyon.

"The miners hurried back to Longview and mounted a search party. They never found the remains of the creature. But when the group went to check out the cabin, they found more boulders tossed around and the interior completely torn to shreds. To this day, people swear they still see these apemen around here. That's why they named the place where the miners lived Ape Canyon," Dana said, finishing the tale and then turning to her boss. "Ruth, do you think we'd have time to hike over there and take some footage of the area before we leave the day after tomorrow?"

Before Ruth could open her mouth, Phil broke in. "We'll have enough trouble finishing our script as it is, Dana. With the volcano alert in effect, I think we should just take what we've already got in the can and get out of here in the morning. Besides, those miners probably trashed the cabin themselves and blamed it on Big Foot."

There was an uneasy stirring in the group at Phillip's heated response to Dana's story, and Beth couldn't understand the hostility in his voice.

But the blond woman just said softly, in a tone drained of its former animation, "You're probably right, Phil."

"Well, Phil," Ruth put in after a weighted silence, "you are correct about us needing the allotted time to finish up our planned schedule. But let's keep an open mind about Dana's story. Who knows what could be lurking out there? If ever there was a place for weird happenings, this is it."

Beth found herself wanting to turn around and scan the darkness outside the campfire for any hairy shapes. But when she saw that Joshua Hunter was once again staring at her from across the fire, seeming to read her mind, she ruthlessly fought down the urge to look over her shoulder. The last thing she needed tonight was him laughing at her.

Just then, Stuart spoke up. "Dana, as master of ceremonies of this little contest, I want to congratulate you on telling a fine yarn. But I'm sorry to say that I'd have to classify it as a tall tale. Anyone have a *real* ghost story to tell us?"

He paused for a dramatic second, but then rushed on before actually giving them a chance to say anything. "Well then, I guess I'll just have to reveal to y'all the most horrendous and terrifying yarn that ever curled a cowboy's toes. *Mar-doc*. You remember *Mar-doc*, don't you, Josh?"

Oh, he remembered *Mar-doc* all right. Looking over at his father's smiling face, he understood that this was why Stuart Hunter had initiated the story-telling contest in the first place. His father loved reciting that tale—over and over.

"Lord, Dad. Not *Mar-doc* again," Joshua groaned, playing the role of straight man. "I should have known that's where you were leading."

"Now, Josh, I know how you hate to listen to it. I realize you've never gotten over your first experience. I warned you at the time that ten wasn't old enough, but you just wouldn't listen. You've been paying for it in nightmares ever since, haven't you, son?"

"Sure, Dad, sure. It made Vietnam seem like a picnic."

"You were in 'Nam?" Phil seemed to really look at the other man for the first time.

"Yes, I was there," Joshua confirmed.

"So was I. Supply and drop. I flew the big choppers. In and out before they knew we were there was our policy. Never had to fire a bullet and never got hit," he bragged.

Joshua looked at him for a long second before answering. Who was this guy kidding? "Well, I never had to fire, either. I was a medic. Mostly, I ducked while putting guys back together who weren't so lucky."

The two of them dropped into a verbal shorthand, revealing that special bonding linking together people who had shared a life-altering experience. Beth had seen the same thing happen when former Peace Corps Volunteers got together at the university. Something set them apart from other people, even years after the events.

She found herself looking intently at Joshua while the men talked. She knew Phil was forty-one, but she hadn't thought that Joshua was old enough to have been in Vietnam. She mentally raised his age by half a dozen years.

Maybe having been in that purposeless war explained the strange aura that surrounded him—the haunted sadness she sensed in him.

"Well, if y'all want war stories," Stuart Hunter broke in after a few minutes, "I can give you some from Korea that'll give you pause."

"Ah, no, Dad. I think I'd rather hear *Mar-doc* again," Joshua said with a heartfelt sigh.

"If you really insist." The senior Hunter grinned in anticipation, falling into the singsong of an oft-told tale.

"It seems there was a cowboy, back in the days when they went out on the range for months at a time, who was sittin' in a soddie hut, dug out of the prairie in northern Texas. He sat by the fire to keep himself warm, one bitter winter night.

"The tin-pipe chimney he carried from hut to hut stuck out of the soddie, which was dug in a hillock. It carried away most of the smoke, while leavin' most of the heat in the lean-to.

"As the buckaroo sat drinkin' his coffee, his potatoes was cookin' and crackin' in the fire. And all the while, the wind moaned across the plains.

" 'Mar-r-r-doc,' it seemed to groan. 'Mar-r-r-doc,' indeed, it mourned again and again. The cowboy pulled his poncho round about, to ease his chill and to stop the shiver in his spine.

" 'Shade, depart,' commanded the wrangler. These was words his long-dead Granma had told him for protection— wise Irish woman that she'd been.

"The magic seemed to work; the sound stopped and the spuds was bakin' nicely in the flames. The puncher smiled and relaxed . . . till once more, much closer now he heard, 'Mar-r-r-doc . . . Mar-r-r-doc . . . MAR-R-R-DOC!'

"Just the wind, he reasoned. But why was old Jed snufflin' and stompin'? That horse was plumb too tired to move before.

" '*Sombra, vaya!*' the man shouted. These was words his ancient *abuela* had told him, in case a spirit came to call—wise Indian *bruja* that she was.

"Minutes passed. The wind died down. A peaceful calm fell on the soddie. The taters was done—hot, soft, and black. The cowboy was just going to eat one, when up on the lean-to jumped a thumpin', dancin' somethin'. It clicked and clacked. It howled in a laughin', cacklin' undulation.

" 'Mar-doc's here now and Mar-doc's hungry, awful hungry, MAR-DOC IS!'

"Down the chimney with sparks aflyin' came two feet, well, the bones, at least.

" 'Mar-doc's-s-s feet is mighty tired,' hissed that voice, so close somehow.

"The cowboy's teeth, they was achatterin', his hair was raised, and his knees was knockin', but he firmly kicked those bones behind him . . . tossed them to the farthest wall.

"Then amid the embers plopped ribs and thighs and knuckles flyin'.

" 'Mar-doc's bones need somethin' stickin', MAR-DOC's HUNGRY!' drawled the tone.

"The *vaquero* did a hoppin' two-step, kickin' spareribs and tossin' bones, back toward that corner of the soddie, where rested ankles and little toes.

" 'HERE COMES MAR-DOC, MAR-DOC'S HERE! I'M TIRED AND HUNGRY AS CAN BE!' Down the chimney, into the fire, dropped a head. All gleamin' and glowin', its eyes were like saucers—no, like suns!

"In the corner, the bones was stirrin'. They joined a toe, a foot, a knee. The spine, it mended . . . fingers added. Till all them bones leapt together, standin' tall and straight and free.

"Then the head crooned, 'Come hungry body, make us whole.' And that mincin' skeleton danced to the fire, it grabbed the head and put it on.

"The man moaned as he crawled and scrambled. Somehow he reached the door. He left that hut screamin' and rantin'. He left it runnin' and cryin', like he feared he might be dyin'.

"Mar-doc, whole now, watched him flyin'. With those eyes still glowin', he shook his head. Then he stretched his bones and ambled over to the fire.

"A bony finger stirred the embers, it raked the spuds, all black and swollen. Popping them in, one by one, Mar-doc cracked their skin between strong jaws.

" 'Thanks, cowboy, the food's real fillin'. The coffee's hot, and the fire's warm.'

"Then most discreetly, he picked his teeth. And when he lay next to the coals, he yawned and slept till dawn."

Stuart reached forward and again stirred the blazing campfire with a dead branch. The logs spat a cascade of sparks that crackled loudly. Along with the rest of the enthralled audience, Beth leaned forward, waiting expectantly for the resolution of the story. But Stuart just surveyed their small group, and then resumed his inspection of the fire.

Seconds passed, a minute. The wind hummed an eerie tune through bare pine trees, and Stuart still didn't say a word.

Finally, Ruth could stand it no longer. "Don't tell me that's all there is! Nothing else? Well, Josh, I can certainly see what terrified you all these years."

She laughed along with the rest of her crew as they all realized that their collective leg had been pulled.

"Nobody ever believes me," Joshua complained. "I feel just like Cassandra must have."

Stuart chuckled happily. "I'll be right back," he assured the group before getting up and walking to his tent. He reappeared a few seconds later with a large transatlantic battery-powered radio. "Since no one can possibly top my story, let's see if we can get some oldies, but goodies to dance to." He fiddled with the dials until he found a station to his liking.

Then pulling Ruth to her feet, he led her into a slow fox-trot played by one of the big bands of the forties. "Remember this one, Ruth?"

"Sorry, Stu, a bit before my time," she chided him, obviously enjoying being in Stuart's arms as she put her head on his shoulder.

Beth started when Phil suddenly loomed over her. "Come on, dance with me," he ordered. When she didn't move and just stared up at him, his voice tightened with sarcasm. "This was supposed to be our engagement party. Or don't you want to be in my arms, either? Is there someone else you'd rather be with?" He didn't look in Joshua's direction, but his meaning was clear.

Beth sighed, but didn't say a word in her defense. She would have it out with Phil in the morning. No use ruining everyone else's night, she thought, rising to her feet and allowing him to pull her into the closed circle of his embrace.

His breath was hot on her neck, and when he began dancing, Beth was surprised that he staggered slightly. He had apparently helped himself to more than his share of the wine while Stuart had been engrossing them in the ridiculous doggerel of *Mar-doc*.

"Phillip, let's sit down!" She tried to pull him toward the fire, but she found that he had other things on his mind. Yanking back on her, his far-superior strength pressed her body tightly against his.

His mouth nibbled her neck and then he whispered, "You're mine, Beth. Nobody else is going to get you and don't forget it." Matching his hands to the words, he began a slow, deliberate exploration of her body.

Beth managed to keep his wandering hands respectable as they danced closer to the other couples, but Phil seemed intent on demonstrating his claim on her so that there would be no doubt of it to anyone.

When they turned near Joshua and Dana, Beth could see that the geologist didn't seem to be enjoying his partner's behavior, either. The blonde was moving just in front of him with exaggerated hip movements more suitable for a rumba than a fox-trot; her eyes beckoned hotly, challenging Joshua to take her up on what was promised in them.

His expression was cold and patronizing, matching the harsh smile that was frozen on his mouth. When he saw Beth watching him, his features lost even the ghost of pleasantness and hardened with anger.

If Beth hadn't been so uncomfortable about the whole situation, she would have burst out laughing at the look on Joshua's face. Surely he wasn't upset that a beautiful woman like Dana was interested in him. Few men would find that exhibition hard to take; Phil was now watching her undulations with ill-concealed fascination.

Perhaps Joshua just didn't like women in general. Beth

shook her head at that wayward thought. She found it hard to believe that he had any masculinity problems. She had no doubts that he had reacted to herself on a man-to-woman level when he tended her wounds that afternoon. And nature certainly wouldn't have wasted all those delicious-smelling male pheromones she had noticed when he had been so close to her.

In the middle of her puzzled thoughts, Phil jerked her close again, showing annoyance at her lack of attention. That was it! Beth had had enough of his manhandling and angrily stomped on his toes.

"Jesus!" he hissed. Surprise, hurt, and rage mingled on his face as the dance ended. Phil dropped Beth's hand in disgust. "Think I'll try someone who enjoys being in a man's arms," he taunted, moving toward the other couple.

Joshua relinquished Dana with a formal nod, and just like Phil had predicted, that statuesque woman molded herself to his body.

Beth stood watching the entwined pair long enough to confirm the fact that she felt absolutely no jealousy. When she moved back toward the campfire to sit down, a large, warm hand turned her by the shoulder. She looked up into enigmatic eyes.

"I don't want to dance anymore," Beth grated through clenched teeth with uncharacteristic rudeness.

"I don't want to dance with you, either. But it seems that I don't have any other choice." His equally cutting reply made her gasp.

Then his strong arms insistently pulled her toward his hard body. Beth tried to hold herself stiffly, fighting the feeling that somehow she had come home. A second later she gave up the struggle, thinking how strange it was that they should fit together so well. When she had danced with Phil just now, she had felt too short. Joshua held her so that their bodies meshed beautifully. The top of her head might have just reached his shoulder, but her forehead found a hollow that seemed designed for her exclusive comfort.

Some of her body tension drained away as she responded to the rhythms of the music, but Beth's mind still was in a swirl of confusion. She knew why the sight of Phil and Dana pressed together in an erotic pas de deux had provoked embarrassment, not jealous rage. But why had Josh's cruel words a minute ago caused her such pain? She had known the man less than three hours.

The song ended and Beth knew she should pull out of Joshua's arms. Instead, she felt the strong fingers gently rubbing the soft hair at the back of her neck, and she found it utterly impossible to move away before the next tune started.

A moment later, the mellow sounds of Glenn Miller's band were instantly recognizable in the sad, slow rendition of "Sentimental Journey" that murmured from the radio.

Joshua drew Beth nearer, nestling her right hand against his chest. With her fingers spread against his solid body, she noticed the smooth texture of his Pendleton shirt, even as she absorbed the warmth of his palm.

It seemed that all her senses had become finely tuned. Her awareness of his clean, masculine scent made her nose twitch. The virile fragrance caused havoc with her brain, evoking a wayward longing in her to taste the taut skin that disappeared into the veed opening of his wool shirt. With her eyes focused on that sun-darkened patch, she fought her desire with all the concentration in her power.

She hardly noticed that the light from the campfire had dimmed. When she finally looked around, Beth found Joshua had danced them well beyond its glow, out of sight of the other two couples.

Fighting panic, she tried to pull away to return to the group. Then in the next instant, Joshua lowered his head and placed his cheek against her hair. He rubbed his skin against it, seeming to enjoy the feel of her soft curls. The gesture arrested any thought she might have had to escape from his embrace.

In truth, she knew that they weren't really dancing anymore, but rather were swaying against each other in a slow seduction of thigh against thigh, body against body.

When Beth looked up and her large tawny eyes searching his face, Joshua found himself sinking into irises that were dilated into huge black pools by the dusky light. He felt her shudder and could sense the heat building just beneath her satiny skin.

With a strange groan, Joshua forcefully pulled his gaze from hers and tried to fault some feature of her gamin face. The smooth cheeks? The pert, straight nose? Her full, ripe lips? He found nothing less than beautiful.

Why now? he silently shouted. *Why on this wretched mountain of all places?* He felt like a marionette on a string. Some force outside himself had made him take her into his arms to dance a few minutes ago. Now, that same controlling hand bent his head and guided his lips toward hers.

"Damn it to hell!" he managed to mutter just before his mouth captured hers in a kiss that shook him to the core. At the touch of her petal-soft lips, a large crack formed in the rigid barrier of indifference that had imprisoned his masculinity for more than a decade.

Although he didn't realize it, the kiss was equally devastating to Beth. Not because it was harsh or forceful, but because it was so sweet and somehow so innocent. She knew that she shouldn't respond; yet how could she not? Especially when she had the crazy notion that he hadn't kissed a woman in a long, long time.

That would explain why he was shaking with such urgency. It would account for the fact he didn't seem to know how to keep his nose from bumping into hers. He didn't even remember that after lips pressed together, they were supposed to soften and open.

Even with that thought in her mind, the novice disappeared and the character of Joshua's kiss transformed. It was as if he had recaptured his misplaced expertise on a surging wave of memory. His mouth became bold and knowledgeable; his tongue delved deep and wicked.

Beth should have been frightened by the way his mouth devoured hers. But instead of pulling away and running for the safety of the campfire, her body played traitor to her will. The hands she had raised to push him away found his thick, vital hair. And though a protest formed in her mind, it never left her trembling lips. Instead, her mouth avidly accepted his searching tongue. Her own tongue needed to probe his dark secrets.

Lord, what is happening to me? Beth barely heard the small island of sanity in her brain. That was because the rest of her body was drowning in the wave of chaos generated by rushing blood and rampaging hormones.

Paradoxically, even in a rising tide of sensual bliss, she actually felt like crying, because this would be their only kiss. She could hardly bear the thought that after this one incredible embrace, she would never feel these arms again. She had finally found the man who could make her forget her deep-seated fears and she would never see him again after this night.

Still under the control of some master puppeteer, Joshua found that his fingers wouldn't stop rubbing the silken strands of Beth's hair or keep from caressing the incredible velvet of her nape.

He knew he was losing control when his hands moved downward to make an intimate survey of her hips. But why didn't *she* break away? Didn't she recognize the danger of letting him hold her so closely? Yet in the next instant, the citadel he had constructed so many years ago crumbled even more. His trembling hands cupped her delightfully round bottom and molded her against the rising need he hadn't acknowledged for so long.

Beth groaned out loud, shocked and shaken by the absolute knowledge of his virility and of his desire. Yet, she made no effort to break free.

Instead, without thinking of the consequences, she captured his head between her hands and initiated a desperate kiss of her own, reveling in the rich taste of his mouth.

Her breath came in ragged, short gasps when he finally pulled his lips off hers. Incredibly, in the dim light, she saw a triumphant grin on his face. She was also surprised to find a deep dimple in his cheek which took years off his face. With its appearance, Beth realized Joshua was really smiling for the first time since they met.

"I don't think you're going to marry that man, Beth . . . ever," he assured her in a low growl. "He's never tasted the kind of kiss you just gave me. You'd better find yourself someone else. Someone who can match the kind of passion you have in you. Price hasn't a clue."

Marry? What was he talking about? Beth's confusion lasted until she had taken several deep breaths. *Phil! He thinks I want to marry Phil.* Embarrassed at how she had just behaved with him, Beth answered without really thinking.

"So, are you offering yourself as a substitute?" *What an egotistical maniac!* she thought to herself. Beth wiped her hand savagely across her mouth, hoping it would erase the impact of her response to him. Yet she still leaned against him. She still allowed his hands to caress her hips as he pressed all of her small body against the long line of his.

"No, not me, Beth." He laughed brokenly. "Sorry, I can't accommodate you. You're just not my type. I was only trying to prove to you that you've been wasting yourself on Price. I know he's never made you feel like this."

Yes, that's the real reason I did this, Joshua rationalized wildly. Still, when he released his hold on Beth's body, he couldn't help running his hands up it to her face and then giving her the gentlest of kisses.

Feeling his long fingers leave a trail of burning need, Beth groaned out loud, totally ashamed of her response to him. Acting on instinct, she struck out at him with a windmilling blow that completely missed its mark. He moved under her clenched fist, easily wrapping her in some sort of entrapping judo hold.

"Never try that on a former Green Beret, sweetheart."

Chuckling into her hair, Joshua gave her one more sweet, slow kiss, which left her in a breathless fury. But before she could think of a suitable retort, he turned her around. With a comradely arm around her shoulder, he guided her back into the campfire.

Stuart and Ruth were drinking coffee, talking and laughing as they sat near the blaze. Beth's eyes searched, but Phil and Dana were not in the clearing.

Ruth looked up. A smile played at the corners of her mouth when she saw them. Somehow, what she observed, looking from her former student to Joshua and back again, seemed to please her inordinately.

At that instant, Beth became aware of the heavily muscled arm still on her shoulder. She shrugged it away and glared at Ruth. This only served to amuse her friend further, and the woman's smile broke into open glory.

"Pull up a section of dirt, brush off the ashes, and have some coffee," she suggested.

"Ruth, where are Dana and Phil? I'm tired and I want to get back to our camp."

"Ah . . . I don't know where they've gotten to. But you shouldn't go off alone. Josh, why don't you walk with Beth? She knows the trail, and Stu will escort me later. Then you both can come back here together."

"That's right, son, I'll meet you over at their camp in a while," his father confirmed.

Beth couldn't think of a graceful way to refuse in front

of the older people. They obviously wanted to be alone. Joshua had already found a flashlight, so with a curt good-bye, she left the compound with him. Stomping angrily along the narrow trail, her muscles felt almost rigid from trying not to brush against the lean man next to her.

The return to her camp seemed to take forever with Beth testing each step. She didn't want to stumble. Joshua already had a low opinion of the command she exerted over her feet. Then in the next instant, she found that only the sulfur-laden air was supporting her body—for the fraction of a second it took for gravity to exert its implacable force.

"Damn, damn, damn," Beth cursed softly to herself, pounding her fist against the earth where she had landed. "Of course, I completely forgot that Murphy's law is in full force on this blasted mountain."

It seemed that the infuriating axiom had put a confounding dip in the trail. Rubbing her bruised ankle, her swearing grew louder and more inclusive.

"Tsk, tsk, tsk. Such language!" When Joshua bent down to scoop Beth up, the superior look on his face in the flashlight's glow made her hit out to keep him away.

"Get your hands off me! I can manage by myself," she informed him, struggling to her feet. Beth balanced on her good leg until the other one stopped throbbing enough to bear some weight.

"Why do I feel a sudden attack of déjà vu?" Joshua asked no one in particular. "Hey, don't be stubborn, Beth. Let me help you. In fact, you've probably been in great need for years of someone to count your change and cut your meat! Look how you keep injuring yourself, look at the man you're involved with." He laughed at his own wit.

"Dr. Hunter," she glared icily at him, "I've been on my own since I was eighteen. I didn't need anyone's help when I put myself through college. I'm doing very well in my chosen profession. I've gotten along without your aid in the past and will do so in the future. Especially in the matter of planning my wedding. I'll even be able to handle the small detail of deciding who the groom will be!" *And no one on this blasted mountain is remotely qualified,* Beth thought angrily to herself. She started a slow hobble down the path, but was finally forced to accept Joshua's hand under her shoulder.

"I just don't understand how you could pick that guy, Beth." He seemed unable to leave the subject. "OK, I'll grant that you may be capable in other areas, but you've made one hell of a mistake in judgment."

His obvious concern, and the fact that she had been thinking something similar herself, made Beth stop to stare up at him. "Just what makes *you* such a good judge of character?"

"I don't know, maybe I was born with it." He thought about it a second. "Or maybe I developed it during my time in Vietnam. You really had to pick your buddies over there or you were dead meat. And as you can see, I'm still here."

"Well, so is Phil!"

"There's nothing wrong with his choice of a . . . buddy. Just yours, Beth."

Beth gave him a sidelong glance to see if the smile on his face was mocking or sincere. She couldn't tell.

"You just met him; how can you be so definite about someone you've only known two hours?" Her voice was a study in exasperation. It had taken her six months to figure out that Phil had serious problems.

But Joshua answered her vexation calmly. "There's just something about him that triggers all sorts of mental alarms. He says he was never shot at in a supply chopper. Ha! Are you sure that he really *was* in Vietnam?"

"Of course he was!" She was certain about that. . . .

Beth had picked Phil up for one date and stopped by

his apartment briefly. In the few minutes she had been there, she had glimpsed a number of photographs he had hanging on the wall of him and other soldiers. She also vaguely remembered a plaque with some sort of military commendation. Phil had been in Vietnam all right.

"Oh, I don't know why I'm listening to you," Beth exploded. "I have no doubts about *your* character, Mr. Magnanimous! You demonstrated it vividly, a few minutes ago. So, just forget about Phil and me. Please feel free to pretend that we've never met. I'll be doing the same."

She raised a defiant chin and negotiated the last two hundred yards to the campsite, allowing only the slightest contact with Joshua's supporting hand.

The arc from his flashlight swept the area when they finally got there.

"Which is your tent?" he asked, and then lit the way to the one she indicated.

When they reached it, the encompassing beam revealed Phil and Dana kissing passionately in the dead trees beyond.

Long seconds elapsed before they became aware of the light and sprang apart, Phil, with a challenging, resentful look on his inebriated face, Dana, as cool as could be.

"Hi, honey." Phil waved as he made his way to his own tent. "I've been kissing a real woman," he mocked before stumbling inside.

Dana nonchalantly ambled over and zipped the flaps down. "Wouldn't want him to catch cold." She smiled lazily, then went to her tent, slipped in, and closed the fabric.

Beth's face burned with a furious fever. She couldn't care less what they did together, but their combined rudeness—their combined cruelty—still had felt like a slap in the face.

She pivoted abruptly toward her own shelter, sending a shooting pain through her ankle that almost buckled her leg. At the sound of her gasp, Joshua reached out and swept her up into his arms. This time, Beth didn't protest, even when he carried her into the tent.

Inside, he sank to his knees and carefully put her on the opened sleeping bag. Beth was too surprised to object when he turned off the flashlight and lay down beside her.

Long fingers began stroking her hair and his deep voice crooned softly in her ear.

"Don't cry, Beth. He's drunk. He didn't mean what he said. A man would be crazy not to want you."

The deep groan Joshua uttered as he captured her mouth seemed designed to reassure Beth of her desirability to at least one appreciative male. But it had the opposite effect. Hearing the muffled moan, all the anger that had been building inside Beth since their first encounter in the afternoon boiled out of her. Struggling fiercely, she managed to pull her mouth away from his, though she was unable to wrench out of his arms.

"Get out of here, you bastard. Don't you patronize me." She lowered her voice to a hoarse rasp, trying to keep her fury from spilling out of the tent, into the silence of the camp. "I don't need your pity, or anything else that's offered. Any man would want me . . . ha! You told me not a half hour ago that I'm not your type. Well, you better find the lucky lady quickly, mister because you're obviously in great need if *I* turn you on like this."

She was tempted to lift a knee into the hard male part of him that was pressing against her thigh.

His reply was amazingly calm. "Don't yell at me because you're angry at Price, Beth."

"I'm not angry with Phil," she protested. And strangely, she really wasn't any longer. She could understand his motivation if he truly thought that he was in love with her. "He was just trying to make me jealous. *He* was mad because I didn't agree to marry him."

Her anger had abated. With its ebbing, she almost

smiled. Here she was, lying in the dark, talking about her relationship with one man while locked in the arms of another.

"Beth, aren't you the least bit jealous of how he was dancing with Dana or the way he was kissing her? Looked to me like he was enjoying it."

"No, I can't say it bothered me, and I told you why." She didn't need to repeat herself.

"Doesn't that give you a clue about your real feelings for him? I think you'd better reconsider any deeper involvement."

"I know exactly how I feel about Phillip," she grated. "I also know just what I think of you. Now, get out of this tent before Ruth and Stuart arrive. I don't need to be embarrassed again in front of her."

"Oh, I think Ruth would understand why I'm here. Smart lady, Ms. Ruth Murray. I can see why my dad was instantly taken with her."

"That's *Dr*. Murray, in case you didn't know. I gather she's your father's type?"

"Definitely, I'd say."

"Well, good luck to the both of them. Look, I'm exhausted and I really wish you would leave. Can't say it's been fun, but it sure was interesting. If you're ever in Los Angeles, please do me a favor: stay away from Westwood and the UCLA campus." Again, she tried to disengage from his embrace.

He didn't let her move an inch. "Funny you should mention that. I'm teaching a graduate seminar there this summer. But I'll try to avoid the biology department, if that's what you want. Goodbye, little girl," Joshua whispered. "You're right, I really should leave before I embarrass you any further."

Beth couldn't help lifting her lips to the light kiss he offered in farewell. It was a bad mistake.

Somehow, that chaste kiss escalated into a deep, probing exploration of each other's mouths. And suddenly, Joshua's hands were everywhere. Yet Beth didn't object when his long fingers ran under her heavy sweater, or even protest when they encountered her small, bare breasts. Instead, she thrilled to the knowledge that his whole body had begun to vibrate when he discovered that she was braless.

His shaking hands covered the firm, rounded mounds, but Joshua was in control enough so that his calloused fingertips were gentle. They stroked the smooth pebbles that were Beth's nipples, causing them to grow full and ripe.

Easing the thickness of her sweater up, he lowered his head to one of those expectant buds, brushing his lips back and forth.

Beth gasped when the cold night air first hit her flushed skin, but she was soon oblivious to that slight discomfort. She became lost in the sharp sensations of Joshua's mouth sucking and of his tongue circling the erect tip.

Devoid of any visual stimuli in the moonless Mount St. Helens night, Beth's world became an arena of gentle caresses and the musky scent of masculine desire.

Needing to touch him, too, her hands tugged at Joshua's Pendleton wool shirt until it pulled out of his jeans. When she brushed his bare back, the hard muscles flexed under her caress, causing currents of sexual electricity to run along the inner surfaces of her fingers.

Then the rough sound of a zipper rasping downward awakened her to what she was doing with this virtual stranger.

"No! Oh, God, please, Joshua. We've got to stop," she sobbed.

For a bittersweet eternity long fingers continued to caress her round bottom through the fragile barrier of lacy silk. Beth's resolve was crumbling fast when Joshua shuddered and his hand stilled.

Abruptly, he moved away from her.

"You're right, this can't go anywhere. You and I both know it," he rasped. "We have to pretend it never happened and that it didn't mean a thing. We have to forget each other. Go ahead, marry Phil, marry anybody. But please, whatever you do, don't come near our campsite again."

Beth refused to answer, to think, even to listen to the fumbling sounds of Joshua moving around the tent. She squeezed her eyes shut at the unexpected glare of his flashlight.

Somehow, she managed not to react when he carefully stripped the used bandages off her elbows. She couldn't help cringing when he placed his lips on the undamaged inner crease of each one or when he stroked a light caress across her damp, curling hair.

A few seconds later, she was alone in the blackness of the tent, with the memory of recent events threatening to overwhelm her.

Some mechanism in her brain knew that it was time to shut off consciousness, to use the dark night hours for healing. She would face this in the morning. She wasn't a coward. But not now.

Joshua passed one of the scorched sentinel pines that guarded Beth's tent and drove his booted foot into its damaged bark. Ignoring the retaliatory shower of dried needles that arced out at him, he increased the length of his stride, determined to put a safe distance between his traitorous body and the source of his torment.

"Why now?" he groaned. For more than a dozen years, his world had been peopled by shadows. Some, like his father, had a little more substance. All the rest, especially golden-haired, feminine forms, had been safely shunted off into some universe that had no connection with him and his agony.

Oh, he had to admit that keeping aloof from life hadn't been quite so easy lately. The first few years' paralysis had retreated a little and reality was a bit harder to deny. Now, besides working on the project, teaching, and sleeping, he found himself listening to music again. Recently, he had become able to tell the difference between a steak and cottage cheese, and today . . . today, his body had remembered the other half of the human race.

The irony of the whole thing was that he hadn't been tripped up by the willowy Dana. His automatic defenses had done a good job with that lady. Her flaxen-haired beauty didn't have a chance to penetrate the fortress surrounding his feelings.

No, it had been a schoolgirl tangle of arms and legs— the wild, untamed sweetness of tawny eyes and generous lips—that sundered his citadel of caution and rallied his hormones until they ran away with his good sense.

Poor Beth . . . He shook his head in sympathy. She hadn't wanted it to happen any more than he did. But she'd been run over by a freight train of pent-up masculine need. Joshua hoped she'd understand just how little she was to blame for this episode. He wouldn't want her to suffer from even a fraction of the oppressive guilt he woke up with every morning and tried to blank out each night.

The sounds of muted laughter alerted Joshua that his father and Ruth were coming his way, just ahead of him on the trail. With a brief exchange of greetings, he indicated that he would wait for the older man after Stuart had delivered Ruth safely to her tent. He had to reassure himself that his dad understood the situation.

Joshua knew Stuart Hunter was very interested in Ruth Murray and probably would be seeing her after this research trip was over. There was no way Joshua could stop that. With a sudden renewal of the agony he had felt for more than a decade, Joshua wanted to be sure that his father would keep his word and not mention Carol to either woman.

For some reason, Beth's opinion of him had become very important. Even though he wouldn't see her again, Joshua didn't want to imagine what her sweet face would reflect if she learned the truth.

To prevent that from occurring, he was prepared to use emotional blackmail on his father to ensure his silence.

____ FOUR ____

Beth's eyes blinked open when the automatic clock in her head rang its silent alarm. With a groan, she turned away from the ray of morning sun that streaked a bright line across her face. The cheerful golden beam that had invaded a chink in the fabric was totally out of place in the tent; it didn't match the bleary-eyed depression she felt.

Don't think about it, she warned herself. Yet she couldn't stop the memory of gentle hands stroking her face and hair or block out the unique male scent that lingered in the air. By allowing that much to surface, a groundswell of emotion rushed over her, and remembrance challenged reality.

She relived those passionate minutes again, feeling the burning, exciting kisses. Her cheeks flamed as she recalled the sensual feelings Joshua Hunter had led her to, for the first time in her life.

Beth had waited so long to find a man who could stir her, she had almost come to believe that she was incapable of passion. Why had it happened now—with Joshua, who

65

professed to have no feelings for her? Why had she almost made love to a stranger?

To her eternal mortification, Beth knew that it was Joshua who had really pulled back at the end. He had kept her from making a complete fool of herself. She had been seconds away from giving in to the sensations he alone had ever made her feel.

It didn't matter that Phil had initiated the sequence of events by his actions with Dana Clark. No, what had happened in her tent last night had occurred because *she* had raged out of control.

The warnings of her brain and conscience had been insignificant compared to the need Joshua's kisses had provoked in her. His caresses had driven her to total abandon in a few short minutes.

Against her will, details of the previous evening impinged on her thoughts again. Beth ran her fingers over the slick nylon covering of her sleeping bag, where Joshua had lain with her. She remembered the feel of *his* fingers as they gently touched her. She shivered at the thought of the roughness of his skin and the softness of his caress. Oh, how easily he had aroused her!

Phil had never made her feel like that, although he truly was as handsome as Josh. Not an inch separated the two men in height, and Phil's body was just as muscular. Yet he'd never once made her experience the wild surge of passion Joshua Hunter's first kiss provoked.

Rubbing her head to ease the pain, Beth knew that she would never see that man again, but she would have to search for his face in every crowd in the future. *Damn him; damn Phil; and double damn me*, she raged.

Sounds of the others getting up for the day's work roused Beth out of her introspective fugue. She would have to talk to Phil. She had to make him understand that she had no intention of going out with him again—let alone marrying him on Saturday.

Using purposeful activity to dampen her depression, Beth pulled on fresh clothes from her kit. Then taking out two large bandages from her catchall cosmetic bag, she carefully applied them to her elbows. They ached, but showed no signs of infection, thanks to Joshua's careful ministrations. Giving one last heartfelt sigh of regret, Beth unzipped her tent and went out to deal with the morning.

She almost fell back into the enclosure to avoid bumping into the woman who waited outside, her beautiful face a study in conflict.

"Oh! B-Beth . . . you're up," Dana stuttered, and then just stared at the ground.

Beth noticed the flare of red highlighting her cheeks and she saw that Dana looked different in a subtle way. Beth examined her face, trying to figure out the change in the girl. She seemed more complex, somehow less open and carefree than she had been in the few days they had worked together. Last night's rude bravado was gone. Dana was carefully avoiding Beth's eyes.

"Did you want to see me about something?" Beth finally asked after long seconds went by.

Dana slowly raised her head to meet Beth's curious gaze. "Yes, yes, I did. Beth, please forgive me for acting like such a bi-witch last night. I don't know what happened to make me behave so cruelly toward you. I realize you and Phil have been dating, and I never, ever poach. God, I don't know . . ."

Beth suddenly understood. Dana was attracted to Phil. She raised a comforting hand to the taller woman's shoulder.

"Forget what happened, Dana. It's every woman's right to make a fool of herself over a man at least one time in her lifetime." Beth grimaced wryly. She had done just that herself last night with Joshua Hunter.

"That doesn't excuse what I did. I tried to get Phil to notice me by dancing like a hussy with Josh. Then I made

Phil leave you at the Hunters' campsite to walk alone with me back here. I even used the fact that he was a bit tipsy to entice him to kiss me. All the while, I knew damned well that the two of you . . ."

"Dana. Although I haven't had a chance to talk to Phil yet, just let me assure you that there is no 'two of us.' We are not a pair. We only dated a few times and he's free to see anyone he wants to."

"Really?" Dana's face lit up. Then it crumbled almost as quickly. "Not that it will do *me* any good. All he can see is you. God, Beth, it's so hard. I mean, I really like you. Who wouldn't? You're so friendly and peppy and smart. But damn, I'm so jealous of you, of the way you earned a Ph.D., while I had such a hard time just getting my bachelor's degree. And the way you look. I feel like a moose beside—"

"*You're* jealous of how *I* look?" Beth interrupted Dana in utter disbelief, gazing up at the beautiful woman. "You don't know it, but I bugged my parents for years to get me those growth hormones so that I could be tall, like my three gorgeous sisters. Who, by the way, resemble you an awful lot."

Dana looked dumbfounded for a second before she started to giggle. Beth found herself joining in.

"The grass is always greener . . ." they said in the same breath and then broke into laughter again.

"Hey, let's go get breakfast started, Dana," Beth suggested when she finally wound down. "I've got a ton of work to do today and have to stoke the old furnace." She rubbed her growling stomach.

"Now, that's another thing," Dana said with a smile. "If I ate a quarter of what you do . . ." She gave her generous hip a whack. "Well, what would happen is too horrible to describe out loud."

Walking over to the propane-fueled cookstove, Beth noticed that the two other members of the crew were moving around the camp clearing. Ruth was uncharacteristically quiet, with a little smile that tended to curl the outer edges of her lips every few seconds while she prepared the coffee.

Phil was even more subdued. After a quick, embarrassed glance at Beth and Dana, he sat down by the stove and began making piece after piece of toast over the gas flame, turning the bread rapidly with a fork.

Beth watched him toast six, ten, twelve slices. "Wait, Phil, that's enough! There are only the four of us, not an army."

"Don't yell, Beth. Please don't yell." Phil put his sore head between his hands, as if trying to block out hurtful sounds from his hung-over brain.

Automatically, Beth went to him and patted his shoulder. But when he tried to put his arms around her, she quickly moved away. "Phil, could I talk to you for a minute after breakfast?" she said distinctly into the quiet morning air.

From a few feet away, both Ruth and Dana looked at her for a long moment. Phil's head jerked up, hope and trepidation warring on his features.

Poor Phil, she thought. *And Poor Dana. What a mess for everyone!*

The smell of burning bread shattered the group tableau. Beth leaned over to rescue the toast. She then located their frying pan and layered bacon into it. After the meat cooked, its delicious smell overcoming the ever-present tinge of sulfur in the air, Beth placed the pieces to drain on paper toweling. Then she poured most of the pan drippings into a small screw-top jar.

Leaving a little grease in the utensil, she mixed powdered eggs with water and scrambled them—frying the result in the fat, which helped take away their awful, processed taste. The mundane actions gave Beth time to get a firmer control of her oscillating emotions.

When Dana handed her the group's metal eating utensils to fill with food, she threw Beth a quick, friendly smile. *How strange we human beings are*, Beth thought when she saw Dana look longingly at Phil. Dana wanted him so badly, while Phil was fixated on Beth. And, although she'd like to deny it, Beth had to admit that she felt an almost overwhelming attraction to Joshua Hunter. The man who had announced loudly to her—and anyone else in hearing range on the volcano's slopes last night—that *she* just wasn't his type.

Lord! This whole crazy tangle was playing like an avante-garde *Midsummer's Night Dream*.

When she caught Dana covertly examining Phil again, Beth wondered how the tall girl could prefer him to Joshua. Didn't Dana understand how grossly she overestimated Phil's appeal compared to Joshua's?

Beth immediately chastised herself for the cruel idea. Maybe love was truly a reaction to body chemistry. Maybe Dana's chemicals were attuned to Phil's. Perhaps her own were designed to match only with those of Joshua Hunter.

It would certainly help explain her abandon last night and why she had never reacted to any other man like she had to him. Beth shook her head. She was just trying to rationalize away her embarrassment.

Not that it mattered. Joshua had already warned her that he was not interested in her. Obviously, her chemicals didn't attract him.

"Oh, Beth." Ruth broke into her rueful thoughts. "I should have asked you to cook up some more bacon and eggs. They should be here any moment."

"They?"

"Stuart and Joshua. They're coming for breakfast. I don't know what happened to them, they should be here already. Why don't you divide up my portion and then I'll make some more food when they arrive. Go ahead and eat yours while it's hot."

For perhaps the first time in her life, Beth felt her appetite depart. She found herself sputtering for a minute, unable to put two words together to tell Ruth what she thought about the idea of sharing another meal with that man.

But when a quarter hour passed with no sign of the Hunters, Ruth reluctantly decided that they had been seriously delayed. Instead of making more eggs, she just buttered a slice of toast and ate the bread with one eye glued toward the direction of the Hunters' camp.

"Well, crew," she finally broke the uneasy postbreakfast silence sometime later, "I guess they're not coming. So let's get to work and discuss today's shooting. It's our last full day and we've got a rough agenda. Just before breakfast, I talked on the radio with our Geological Survey friends in Vancouver. Their helicopter is on a really tight schedule and we can't extend even an hour beyond our original plans. Tomorrow we can do a little mopping-up action, redoing a couple of scenes we flubbed. Then we have to be at the pickup point by three." She turned to Beth. "Honey, I'd like you to go back to that lahar, a quarter mile south of here. Remember the mudflow where we saw the ants two days ago?"

Beth nodded; she recalled the lahar site.

"I'd like you to get some close-ups of the warriors, along with the workers. If we can intersperse the stills with the footage Phil took, I think the effect will be overwhelming. I've decided to change the thrust of the film. Everything we've taken supports it. I don't know why I didn't see it before. It all seemed to gel in my mind last night."

"Ruth, for heaven's sakes, what *is* the theme?"

Beth and the others laughed at their boss's habit of taking a very roundabout path when making a point.

"Oops, sorry, did it again, didn't I?" She grinned before going on. "My idea is: for everything, there is a season. You know—from Ecclesiastes. I can't remember the whole thing. All I can recall is, 'There is a time to be born and a time to die; a time for war and a time for peace; a time to love and a time to hate.' I'm not even sure of the order. Any of you know the section?''

None of the others could come up with the exact wording, either.

"Oh, well, I'll look it up when we get back. But that's what we're going for, that contrast. Everything we've done so far fits it beautifully.''

"That sounds exciting, Ruth. How did you think of it?'' Beth asked.

"It was something Stuart and I were talking about last night.'' After looking in the direction of the Hunter campsite once more, Ruth's usually merry green eyes became serious. "We were discussing life and lost love and the effect separation has on people. Light stuff like that,'' she finished with her usual nonchalance.

Beth wasn't fooled. Ruth was disturbed by something in the late-night conversation she and Stuart Hunter had shared. She would get it out of her boss when they were alone.

"Anyway, Beth, you can go along the trail we broke to the mudflow. There hasn't been enough rain or snow since we were there to make the lahar dangerous. I need both Phil and Dana to take some film at the edges of the pyroclastic flow region, north of here. I hope we can get a few grumblings recorded, maybe even a puff of steam. Mixed with stock footage from earlier eruptions, we'll have more than enough film for our half hour.''

Beth looked around the campsite for a minute while the others went to gather their heavy equipment for the day's shooting. Ruth had conferred with government experts about the best place to set up their base camp. They had suggested a point on the lowest slopes of the volcano. It gave the film crew safe access to areas of ash, mudflows, and the rock-runs of the pyroclastic activity of a decade's worth of eruptions.

When they were brought in by helicopter six days ago, the pilot had approached from the south side of the volcano. It had been barely damaged in the 1980 eruption. The Gifford Pinchot National Forest, with its thick stands of tall pines, gave no hint of what was waiting for them on the opposite flank of the mountain.

Passing the southern timberline, the pilot had dipped low. Beth had seen dozens of hikers slogging up the lower slopes, Day-Glo orange runners defining the routes.

After the helicopter swung around to the eastern side of the mountain, the pilot pointed out the barren Plains of Abraham, which Beth recognized from her research.

Then they flew across the border of hell. The crew was hit with the reality of what damage a major volcanic eruption can do to miles of countryside. From the air, nothing green was visible on the northern slopes. Even a dozen years after the first horrible explosion, they looked down on miles and miles of devastation.

Everything was covered by ash to varying degrees. Gray was the predominant color; denuded brown was the contrast. Only the clear blue of the sky above relieved the feeling that she had reached the devil's stamping grounds.

It wasn't until they had landed and set up camp that Beth found a brighter chapter in the Mount St. Helens story.

When she examined the lower reaches of the destruction, she discovered a myriad of signs that life had successfully fought back, that nature was on the march to reclaim what had disappeared amid searing ash and smothering mud.

Anxious to do her part in telling that story, Beth went to her tent to get her own equipment. Her assignment today would be easy. It was only complicated by her slightly aching ankle and the weight of depression she felt on her head. The elastic bandage she had included in her kit would help her foot. She didn't have such a convenient remedy for her bruised soul.

Just as she shouldered her pack, Beth heard a scraping sound outside her tent. She stiffened with apprehension when Phil poked his head inside. He was lugging his light-weight, hand-held videotape camera and film case on his back.

"Beth, I need to talk to you. You have something to say to me, too?"

She nodded, aware that this was something that couldn't be put off any longer. Gathering up her equipment, she then led Phil out of earshot of the others, while still in plain sight of the two women. She didn't want a repetition of yesterday's frightening episode.

"I don't know what happened last night, honey," he began without preamble. "I remember drinking too much and that I hurt you, somehow. But I'm really hazy about the whole thing." He looked at her sheepishly.

"Oh, Phil . . ."

"I don't understand why I took that stuff," he plunged on. "I should know better. I'm actually allergic to alcohol and can't handle even a little. You've never seen me drink before. I've kept away from it ever since I got back from Vietnam. Will you forgive me, Beth?"

She looked up at the blond man, knowing that he was trying to be truthful with her. Beth wanted to be equally frank with him.

"Don't worry, Phil. I'm not angry with you, not at all. For someone who isn't used to drinking, you didn't do anything to worry about. Phillip . . ."

"Beth, about what happened with Dana . . ." he broke in, obviously remembering more than he was admitting. "Oh, she's nice enough . . . a beautiful woman, but she doesn't mean anything to me. I was just trying to make you jealous, little girl. Because you refuse to admit that you love me and that we are going to get married.''

"Phil, I know my own mind, my own heart. Why do you keep thinking of me like a child? I'm twenty-nine, for pity sakes. And I do not want to—"

"Aw, Beth. Don't say it. Please. Let's get down from this blasted mountain before we make any firm decisions. Please, honey.''

Seeing the pain in his pale eyes, Beth almost relented. What difference would a few days make? Perhaps he was right. Away from the almost surreal atmosphere on the volcano, maybe Phil would see that they really weren't right for each other.

Then Beth remembered the agony she had seen on Dana's face. It would be cruel to her, and in the long run to Phil, not to set the record straight right now.

"No, Phil. I can't do that. I like you too much to lie to you, even by omission. I can't marry you . . . ever. You're a wonderful man, but I don't love you.'' She put a hand on his jacket sleeve before the anger she saw on his face could explode into hot words. "Phil . . . we can't help who we love, and I have to believe that there's some-one fine for each of us. We just have to keep looking. Maybe your subconscious was telling you something when you kissed Dana last night.''

"Forget about me kissing Dana. You're the woman for me, Beth, and I'm not going to give you up . . . ever.''

Phil turned abruptly and stalked back toward the others. With her stomach churning out enough acid to generate a world-class ulcer, Beth followed a few steps behind him.

Ruth and Dana had packed their equipment and were waiting for the pair's return, Ruth with obvious impa-tience, and Dana with a tense look on her face. Beth could only give her a helpless shrug. How could she tell the woman that Phil was still refusing to believe that she did not want to marry him?

She had to keep herself from going to comfort Dana when the blonde quickly went to her tent with a mumbled excuse. Beth didn't want to call attention to the suspicious moisture she had seen on the tall girl's cheeks.

Sighing, Beth squeezed her eyes shut for a long second. *Maybe some brilliant plan of action will come to me while walking to my worksite*, she told herself. Opening her eyes, Beth resettled her camera equipment around her neck. She turned in the direction of the ant colony she was supposed to shoot and called over her shoulder, "I'll see you all at lunch."

"Hey, till lunch, honey," Phil echoed, sounding so cheerful that their heated conversation might never taken place. "How about if I get my target pistol and see if I can find us a rabbit? Nothing like fresh meat to fill that hollow little tummy of yours."

He had already turned back toward his tent before Beth could get her voice working around the lump of shock that filled her throat.

"Oh, Phil, don't do that! They've had such a hard time reestablishing. We can all have a big steak back in Portland tomorrow night. All right?" she beseeched, hating the pleading tone in her voice.

Phil pivoted, his mouth curving into a satisfied smile. "OK, Beth. Anything to make you happy, sweetheart. Although I think I'll take the gun for some practice anyway. Got to keep my expert's rating." He laughed and then entered his shelter.

Beth turned to Ruth, who just shook her head.

"You won't let him kill anything, will you, Ruth?"

"Not if I can help it," she assured Beth.

"Good. What time will you return here for lunch?"

"We'd better not make any definite plans. We could be a long time. If you get back before us and are famished, as usual, just go ahead and eat without us." Ruth smiled wryly. Her grin slipped into a look of surprise when the tents of the camp started swaying.

Several of the dried, denuded trees in the vicinity creaked and cracked ominously as a strong earth tremor rocked the area.

High above their level, the broken edge of the volcano's crater emitted a sharp retort and sent a column of steam four or five thousand feet into the air.

"Uh oh! Looks like someone was listening when I asked for fireworks to record," Ruth observed, her freckles very obvious in the sudden pallor of her skin. "Dana, get on the radio and ask USGS in Vancouver if we should be concerned about this activity," she directed her sound technician-cum radio operator after the girl came running out from her tent.

Phil had also appeared, stowing his target pistol in his film case and hurrying toward the women.

Dana broke out the set from its protective covering. She turned to their prescribed band and tried to raise Vancouver, using their call numbers over and over again.

Five minutes later, the government agency finally responded. "This is Vancouver. We read you. What is your situation? Over."

"Vancouver, we have no problem as of the moment. What is the status of Mount St. Helens? We just had a minor event; will it become a major one? Over."

Beth admired Dana's cool, concise stating of the situation. She wondered if her own voice would have been as steady, if she had made the call.

"We're checking. Will contact you within fifteen minutes and advise your situation. Over and out."

"Over and out." Dana shut down the transmitter, leaving on the receiving mode.

"Well, put your stuff down, everyone," Ruth advised. "We have a few minutes' wait. How long do you think it would take us to get our equipment to the pick-up point, Phil?''

Phil was staring at the cloud of steam that was now dissipating at the ten-thousand-foot level above the mountain. A fine rain of ash began to fall, and a sulfurous miasma filled the air.

''Phil?'' Ruth walked to the man and touched his arm.

He started and then turned to reveal a strange expression. Beth was surprised at the tension displayed by his clenched jaws; the muscles were working over the bones and his eyes were slightly disorganized.

''What did you say?'' he asked Ruth, turning back to the mountain again. She repeated the question.

''Oh, it'll take about an hour. We'd have to make two trips for the camping supplies and one for the filming equipment, like we did when we back-packed it up to this point six days ago.''

His eyes never left the peak above them as he spoke. The jagged edge bore mute testimony to the force of the explosions that had sent death-bringing flows of super-heated rock, ash, and steam down to Spirit Lake.

When the volcano had first reawakened in the huge 1980 eruption, broiling lahars had run to the north and west. The hot mud had mixed with landslides of debris to fill the north and south forks of the Toutle River.

Almost sixty people were known to have perished in that disaster. Beth was very aware that she and the rest of the crew had been working, eating, and sleeping with a time bomb over their heads. At the moment, her nerves couldn't quite believe the geologists, who were almost certain that there would not be anything as monumental as the 1980's eruption for centuries.

They *did* warn that there was a far greater chance for localized events that could produce pyroclastic flow, heated mud slides, and dangerous avalanches. That was why the authorities had cleared the area of tourists and climbers yesterday. Only people like themselves, with valid permits for necessary research, were still on the mountain. Now, even their experienced group was subject to recall.

Phillip began pacing, obviously unable to just wait for the radio report.

"Maybe we should get things ready, Ruth," he suggested. "That would save time if we have to evacuate quickly. The videotape we've already got in the can could be taken down, along with our spare gear and anything else we don't need."

"That's an idea, Phil. Why don't you start separating out the nonessential equipment."

"OK. I'll get on it right away." He almost ran to do what Ruth had asked of him.

She stood there, shaking her head. Beth was equally puzzled and concerned by Phil's frenzy of activity. She had never seen him like this. He looked frantic . . . almost terrified.

Her thoughts seemed ridiculous. Surely he had been in situations that were far more grave than a puffing volcano, she reasoned, trying to dismiss her disquieting observations.

"Hello there," a deep, masculine voice suddenly called from the far side of the camp.

"Stuart!" Ruth answered, walking quickly toward the geologist. "Stuart, what in the world happened to you? We expected you an hour ago."

"I'm sorry, Ruth. We forgot to exchange radio call numbers. Something's happened to the laser readings we're getting. The numbers are way off. Josh and I were busy fiddling with the light emitter since dawn."

Beth found herself looking down the trail, trying to see beyond the dust devil that had formed behind Stuart Hunter. She forcefully told herself that she was relieved when there seemed to be no sign of the younger geologist.

"Where's Josh? Didn't he come with you?" Ruth asked

the question that Beth would have bitten off her tongue before expressing.

"Oh, we walked most of the way together. But Josh wanted to take readings at another site, so he went off on another trail about a quarter mile from here."

"Mount St. Helens, come in. This is Vancouver, over." The radio burst into life. The group quickly converged on it, watching Dana switch on the transmitter.

"Vancouver, this is Mount St. Helens, we read you, over."

"Mount St. Helens, you can relax. Our instruments show no magma movement, and harmonic tremors are at a minimum. No imminent eruption is predicted. Keep your radio with you at all times and we'll advise if the situation changes. Repeat, you can go until scheduled pickup tomorrow, at three P.M. The only problem may be a weather cell moving in from the Pacific. Pickup may be earlier because of it. Do you read? Over."

"Vancouver, we read. Pickup may be ahead of schedule. Over and out."

"Over and out." The disembodied voice died. All that remained was a hissing of the radio ether, until Dana canceled that effect by switching off the set completely.

"OK, crew, let's go to work," Ruth said. "You all heard the man; there's no immediate danger. Stuart, do you have to help Josh, or would you like to come along and see a professional film crew at work?"

"Joshua is not expecting me, so I wouldn't miss going with you for the world."

"Beth, why don't you come along, too?" Ruth suggested. "I think it would be better if you're with us."

"Oh, no, Ruth. I really think your idea about the warrior ants is perfect for the new theme. It would be a shame to lose it. I'll be all right. There's only a short distance to go, and you remember how well we marked that trail. See you later."

She didn't give the other woman a chance to protest. Nor did Phil make any move to stop her. He was looking at the mountain again.

Beth quickly shouldered her film and equipment case and hung her camera around her neck. Out of sight of the camp, she stopped for a moment to wrap her ankle with the elastic bandage she had stuck in her pocket. She then put on safety goggles to keep out any stray ash.

An ironic smile tugged at her mouth. She'd really have to be more careful about her health in the future since her personal paramedic wouldn't be making any more tent calls.

FIVE

They had marked the trail to the lahar with pieces of bright-orange biodegradable twine. Beth didn't know if her idea was original or if she remembered it subconsciously from some book. In any case, she was inordinately proud of the little snippets that unerringly guided her back to the spot the crew had previously examined.

Her jaunty mood abruptly dissolved when she reached the mudflow site. Joshua Hunter had already set up his equipment. Beth froze in surprised dismay, unable to retreat. She watched helplessly as the tall man turned and then walked toward her with long strides of his denim-covered legs.

The force of his body's attraction for her produced alarming sensations. Now that she knew its hazards more intimately, the thought of being alone with him made her tremble.

Beth ruthlessly extinguished the glowing flame that his very presence had kindled in her secret depths. There would be no repeat of last night's madness.

"Don't move, Beth. Although I understand that you

can't wait to see me, I've spent an hour on this setup, and I just can't let you knock it down in your enthusiasm.''

Joshua found himself laughing at the look of astonishment on Beth's face. It was such a good feeling, he did it again. The joy he felt at seeing her once more surprised the hell out of him. Last night he had literally felt haunted by the past. He had been so aware of the aura of guilt and sadness flowing around the mountain that he expected to see Carol's spectral form floating overhead.

Yet here in the cloud-checkered morning sunshine, he had to admit that he was damned glad that Beth had found him. He wanted to be in her company, even if it just postponed the minute when he had to say goodbye to her forever.

With Joshua grinning down at her, Beth could see that he wasn't in the least perturbed by what had happened between them yesterday. She couldn't see his eyes, because he again wore those mirrored goggles for protection, but she felt a teasing twinkle behind the lenses nonetheless.

His whole attitude provoked a wide spectrum of feelings within her. Beth alternately bristled in exasperation at his self-centered interpretation of why she was there, then flushed with embarrassment, remembering her abandon with him. Overwhelming these responses was the pure happiness she felt at seeing that big dimpled grin on his face. Appalled at the strength of the emotion, Beth schooled her own features into neutral lines so she could challenge his statements.

"Sorry to shatter your egotistical pipe dreams, Dr. Hunter, but I'm on assignment here and you've put your equipment right in the middle of the ant colony I was supposed to photograph." It was wonderful to finally be able to shift the role of klutz on to Joshua Hunter's broad shoulders.

"Ant colony, where? There isn't a living thing within

a square mile of this place." He searched the space around his boots.

"That shows how much you know. Come here." She impulsively grabbed his hand and dragged him near his setup. He hadn't actually destroyed the area she wanted to work. He had placed his instruments a few feet away from the activity trail she remembered seeing two days ago.

Still clutching his hand, Beth got on her knees. She pulled Joshua down to her level for a change, indicating the march line of ants running along the edge of the old mudflow.

"See . . . see . . . hundreds of workers. Look, they've got pieces of parsley fern to take back to the nest, and that group's captured an ant from another species of *Formicidae* to use as a slave. How can you say there's no life here?" she demanded.

"Where? I don't see anything," Joshua said, peering to where she was pointing.

Exasperated, Beth took off her goggles. Sticking them in a pocket, she reached over to push up his pair on to his forehead.

"No wonder you can't see; these mirrored things must block out nearly as much incoming light as they reflect back."

In pushing them out of the way, she finally found out why it had been so difficult to identify the color of Josh's eyes yesterday; they were a Technicolor combination of shades that changed by the second even as she looked into them.

Surrounding the black center, a rayed ring of gold was in turn encompassed by a larger circle of turquoise, while a thin black annulus completed the iris. The gold area pulsed with his heartbeat; the other layer contracted and expanded with variations too subtle and fleeting to assign a color name.

What beautiful and quixotic eyes . . . just like the man himself, Beth thought. She finally dragged her gaze away, feebly directing his attention back to the labors of the multifooted creatures on the ground.

"I still don't see anything," Joshua persisted.

Beth moved closer to the line, lowering herself so that her chest was flat on the ground. With her chin resting on one fist, she pointed with the other hand.

"Look! Are you blind?"

Joshua lay down with his head next to her pointing finger. He sighted along it and finally said, "Hey, you're right. Look at the buggers go!"

He moved to see better, draping a casual arm around her shoulders while pressing his long body against her side just as nonchalantly.

"Where do these fellows live, Beth? Is their colony above ground, or below?"

His interest seemed sincere, so, dampening her awareness of the hard body stretched out next to hers, Beth answered his questions with a professional naturalist's enthusiasm.

"These *ladies* live underground. They b-burrow down ten or more feet, which is why they have s-survived the various eruptions here, of c-course."

Beth was acutely chagrined at the trouble she was having with articulation. She struggled valiantly to marshal her facts, trying to control her stuttering tongue and give him a coherent lecture on the ants.

"They're at the top of their food chain, you know. Which, of course, suggests that all links down to the lowest level of the ecology must have survived here, in some measure. Or at least, substitutes have been found which allow the colony to flourish after all the eruptions . . ."

Joshua had turned his attention from the march line to her face. Laying his cheek on his right arm, his nose wasn't five inches from her. His gorgeous eyes bore into hers with a sudden, disturbing seriousness. His mouth was just a handbreadth away. Even as she measured the distance, the space got smaller and smaller, until he touched her lips with the gentlest of kisses.

It was a salute that she almost wouldn't have felt, if it hadn't been for the fire it caused to leap in her breast and the stab of ecstasy that traveled from some inner place to shimmer in her brain.

Oh, the devil! Why would he do this again? He had disavowed their attraction for each other last night. Trying to roll away before she revealed any more to him, Beth was captured by encircling arms. He laughed and began nuzzling her neck, ignoring the silent battle she waged attempting to win free.

Her ambivalent feelings warred in her brain. She wanted, with all her heart, to wrap herself like a windswept leaf to the strength of his body, but she wasn't going to do that again.

"Leave me go. I said let go of me. You are no gentleman! You know I don't want this. Have you no morals?"

Joshua pulled his head back, seeming genuinely surprised. "No morals? Me? What about you? You're keeping Price dangling until you find someone more suitable. 'Moral' would be to let him go, to let Dana console him."

There was no way that Beth was going to let Joshua Hunter know that she had ended her tenuous relationship with Phil. That misconception was the only thing that was protecting her from him. And Beth from herself, she reluctantly admitted.

Apparently deciding that her antagonistic silence was caused by his teasing words, Joshua amended, "Dana's better for him, though I'll admit that he only has eyes for you. I guess you were right about last night; he was angry because you wouldn't name the big day. Why not, honey?"

"Why, you . . . you . . ."

He blithely ignored Beth's impotent sputterings. "Could it be that your subconscious is trying to tell you something? Like he isn't the man for you? Hey, I have an idea . . ."

His eyes glowed with sudden inspiration. Before Beth could shout out that she didn't want to hear any of his ideas, he offered her an outrageous plan.

"I'll tell you what: remember that I said I'd be spending the summer in Los Angeles? Well, I'll take you out 'til you find someone better than Price. You won't have to sit at home waiting for Mr. Right. I'll help you scout out the most likely places and protect you from your bad judgment. What do you say?"

Although he grinned cheerfully, Joshua couldn't quite believe what he had just said. In the last dozen years he had fiercely restricted his contact with the gentler sex to only the most necessary interaction. Why was he able to forget Carol for minutes at a time in Beth's presence—and here on Mount St. Helens of all places?

Beth stared at Joshua, not caring that her mouth was opening and closing like a beached fish. She couldn't believe the insensitive gall of the man, offering to provide her with a personal escort service.

"No! Thank you very much, no. I don't ever want to see you again," she finally managed, dismissing his incredible suggestion. "I don't need your help, you big, overgrown clod. Now let me go, I can't stand you touching me!" Her mind registered, but didn't understand the shudder that went through Joshua's muscles at her accusation.

"So you can't bear my touch, hmm?" All of a sudden, that deep voice was full of silky menace.

With no apparent effort on his part, Joshua rolled slightly, his weight pinning Beth.

His face was so close to hers now that Beth couldn't focus on it. She closed her eyes tightly, like a child shutting out what frightens it. However, she had no choice but to listen to him.

"Don't you remember what happened in your tent last night?"

Rotten! He was utterly, unredeemably rotten. Beth moaned as his words reopened a running wound. Misinterpreting her anguished reaction, Joshua's elbows lifted his body to relieve her chest of a bit of his weight. But he didn't release Beth. Instead, he held her face and brushed her lips lightly with his.

Beth forced herself to remain rigid, with her eyes squeezed shut and lips fused closed. However, when the smooth tip of Josh's tongue began stroking a moist trail around its fullness, she opened her mouth to protest. Her attempted challenge served only to permit access to the mutable instrument, which probed the satiny inner tissues with the burning stroke of a jungle cat's caress.

The heat of his tongue kindled hers into answering his deep thrusts with quick, timid darts of her own. With a seductive rumble in his chest, Joshua chuckled at her reaction. Totally vanquished, Beth was past caring that she had exposed her desire to a man who was only trying to prove a point . . . that she couldn't resist his touch.

Even knowing that, all she wanted to do was become part of him.

Confident that she wouldn't pull away now, Joshua rolled on his side to allow himself and Beth more freedom of movement and exploration. Revealing his own intense need, he guided her hands to his shirt, encouraging her to unbutton it and stroke his hot skin.

When she hesitated and her eyes caught Joshua's questioning gaze, she begged in mute supplication for assistance in stopping this madness. But trying to appeal to his character to do the right thing was a mistake. Instead of responding to her silent plea for help, Joshua just began undoing her own shirt.

The nipple of her exposed breast surged into hard prominence at the slight grazing touch of his calloused thumb.

"Look at that, Beth. Are you still sure that you hate my touch?"

"Why are you doing this to me?" she wailed. "Don't you remember what you said to me last night—to marry Phillip, to keep out of your sight?" The memory of those harsh words brought stinging tears of shame to the corners of her eyes.

"Oh, sweetheart. I'm sorry. I must have been crazy to say that to you," he muttered, stroking away the moisture with the tip of his tongue.

Perversely, his gentle words and tender possession only fueled the rage that rebounded through Beth's skull. Yet, there wasn't a physical thing she could do to move him. And her mind was too paralyzed by the cold chill of fury she felt to think of words harmful enough to satisfy her.

In the next second, that iceberg of suppressed anger melted into a puddle of fear. The earth moved beneath Beth in a sickening repetition of the morning's event. Joshua froze and then gathered her against his chest, shielding her body with his own until the tremors subsided.

Passion drained out of the two of them. The reality of the cold, dusty ground beneath—and the possibility of hot, searing death above—put a sudden end to the sensual conflict in which they had been involved.

She mutely looked at him with stricken eyes. Shaking his head, he answered her unvoiced question, "No, I don't think so. Although I came out here this morning because I didn't understand some of the readings the equipment was getting at the base camp. I thought a different location might confirm that nothing big is going to happen here in the near future. Let's see what the instruments show and I'll be able to tell you more."

He gave her one of his slow, sweet kisses, which took

the sting out of his previous actions. Beth somehow knew the caress was not meant to be erotic, but rather as a sincere apology.

Getting to his feet, Joshua held out his hand to help her up. Because both of them needed to block out what had just passed between them, each began carrying out the assignments their impulsive lovemaking had postponed.

Joshua examined the geologic apparatus and began writing down the series of numbers the needles had recorded in the last few minutes; Beth retrieved her camera and found the warrior ants she had come to photograph.

Four times larger than the workers, their armored heads and mandibles made them look like a cross between space invaders and knights errant. In her extreme close-up lens, they were monstrous. She knew that gram for gram, these ants numbered with the fiercest, most efficient killing machines nature had ever created.

Clicking the shutter relentlessly, Beth relied on her high-speed film to catch the quick movements of the warriors. She worked until finally satisfied that she had captured the total power and menace of the creatures. Then putting her camera into its case, she sat down on the ground and waited quietly for Joshua to finish his analysis of the data. He was perched on a rock, alternately checking his notebook and working a pocket calculator.

"Not conclusive," he sighed after a half hour or so. "In fact, these readings either suggest some sort of mechanical error or that my basic formula is full of holes. Although, after testing its accuracy over the last few years on every volcano from Navado del Ruis in Colombia to Mount Pinatubo in the Philippines, I'd bet the rent money that there's nothing wrong with my calculations . . ."

He stopped talking abruptly and stared up at the horseshoe-shaped breach in the mountain's rim. "Mechanical error . . . maybe that's it." He got up and went a few steps to his backpack lying on the ground. Pulling out a two-way radio, Joshua switched it on, and for several minutes, he droned out a series of call numbers.

"Roger, what in the world took you so long to answer?" he almost shouted with relief when the company pilot finally answered.

"We're in the middle of a rescue operation." The tinny sound of a man's voice reached Beth. "There's a major crash on Highway 504. Some tourists tangled with a logging truck . . . a real mess. We volunteered to help clear the road."

"Well, good work, Roger. But I was hoping to take a quick trip to the lava dome. I think something might have happened to a couple of the special reflectors we set up there. Maybe the seals broke and clouded the mirrors. I've been getting screwy readings that are messing up my analysis."

"We'll be tied up for another couple of hours. I could probably get you by two-thirty, maybe three."

Joshua looked over at Beth. "That's OK, Roger. I have enough on my agenda here that I won't have to twiddle my thumbs until then. Say, why don't you bring up a couple of replacement mirror assemblies with you?" He quickly gave Roger the coordinates of his position and signed off.

After stowing the radio, Joshua walked back to Beth. "Our company's helicopter pilot is temporarily based in Vancouver while we're up here. He'll be picking me up in a couple of hours for a trip up the crater."

"So I heard," Beth responded, looking up at the mountain's ruined crest. "I'd really like to see the lava dome up close. Would it be possible to—"

"Absolutely not!" The mere thought of Beth standing on that crumbling rim sent a bolt of cold lightning down his spine. "Don't you know how dangerous it is up there? The USGS closed the crater to climbers months ago because of how the lava dome has been venting. And with all these minor earthquakes . . ."

"Joshua, I'm not a tourist," Beth responded quietly. "I may not have been on a whole lot of volcanoes like you have, but I know how to handle myself in hazardous situations. I was at Yellowstone through that whole summer of wildfires a few years ago. Ruth and I filmed right next to the firefighters on the line. We weren't foolhardy, but we didn't let the danger stop us from making our documentary."

"You and Ruth did a documentary during the Yellowstone disaster?"

"Yes, perhaps you saw it. *Firestorm*. It was pretty widely distributed."

"*Firestorm*! Of course I saw it; most of America did. It was incredible. You and Ruth made that film? Didn't it get an Academy Award?"

"Nominated . . . but we didn't win."

Joshua knew he was being chauvinistic, but he was having the hardest time connecting the two beautiful women he had met yesterday with one of the best documentaries he had ever seen. He remembered thinking at the time that the filmmakers were remarkable. Remarkably brave and remarkably talented. The work had been lyrically poetic, but full of unexpected humor. It had careened along the fire line, figuratively pulling the viewing audience through the screen so that they teetered on the edge of disaster right along with the firefighters.

Lord! Beth had been in the thick of the smoke and flame and exploding trees. Joshua squeezed his eyes shut against the image of her amid the fast-moving conflagration that had destroyed so much of the national park.

Well, she might be a professional, but there was absolutely no way he could take her up with him to the caldera. The very thought of it made him sick.

"What about it, Joshua? Can I tag along on the helicopter?" Beth asked again.

"I'm sorry. You don't have the proper authorization. I also have to caution you from going up there on your own."

Beth was disappointed by his refusal, but it was his helicopter, his call. Looking at the tension on Joshua's face, she saw that he really was concerned for her safety.

"OK, that's all right," she finally said. "I can understand your position . . . insurance and all, even though I *do* have the required permits. If it's so dangerous, should you be going up there, either? What's your gut feeling? Do you think we should pack it in right now?"

Joshua could hardly believe that Beth was handling his refusal so well. He had expected her to explode. Looking down on her lovely face, his opinion of her went up another notch.

"No, Beth, I'm sure you'll be reasonably safe down here. At least for the next day or so. According to the data I got before the instruments went crazy, there will be an event in the next forty-eight to fifty-four hours. But I don't think anything really big is in the works inside the lava tube; the area of danger will be very localized.

"Still, I've stuck my neck out and given the authorities a prediction. That's part of the reason why they've cleared the restricted zone of tourists and nonessential personnel. Everybody else will be out by tomorrow afternoon. So we'll be just fine . . . nobody will be killed this time," he said quietly.

"How can you be so sure?" Beth protested. "I thought several eruptions have occurred, here and other places, that completely fooled the experts."

"Yes, but that was before I developed my formula," Joshua said with such sincerity that it didn't seem like a boast at all. "My theory is based on material stress

breakpoints. You know, like metal fatigue. A given substance—like steel or rock—will always fracture when sub-
jected to a certain amount of force. Every time . . .
guaranteed.

"Since we know quite a lot about the exact composition
of the rocks that make up this mountain, it's possible to
measure the stresses using surface indicators, like gravito-
meters, and tiltmeters, and the laser-reflector array that
I've developed. You see, Mount St. Helens behaves much
like other composite cones . . ."

Joshua went on to explain the technicalities of volcanic
mountain building, giving Beth a concise course. He constructed a vivid mental picture for her, while defining
every term he used in very clear language. Yet, after a
while, Beth found herself letting his voice wash over her,
listening to the quiet confidence of Joshua's tone rather
than to the process he outlined.

"Anyway," he finished, "we're only experiencing
stage-two symptoms. Stage one was earth tremors; stage
two is steam and ash. Three and four—explosion and
magma runs—are usually days later. I'm sure that we have
a wide safety margin if we leave by tomorrow afternoon."

"You must be popular with your students. That was
the best presentation of vulcanism I've ever heard," Beth
complimented him.

He looked startled when he saw the admiration on her
upturned face. "And you've heard this all before, haven't
you?" he challenged her. "Why didn't you stop me? How
many geology courses have you had?"

"Oh, a few. I've always been interested in paleontology, and I took geology to help me put all the eras into
perspective. I wasn't kidding, though, Joshua. I think
you're a fantastic lecturer. I'm sorry I didn't have you for
my instructor."

He looked speculatively at Beth. "Oh, that might be

arranged—for some other subject if not geology." He smiled wickedly, then felt like groaning in embarrassment.

Joshua didn't know what kind of little devil had taken control of his tongue. He hadn't said anything so corny to a female since he was fifteen years old. To make matters worse, he knew that the sudden alteration in the fit of his Levi's revealed just how wayward his thoughts seemed to become around this woman . . . only with this woman.

Feeling her cheeks burn with an absolute knowledge of the direction Joshua's train of thought was chugging to, Beth jumped up and announced in a rush, "Well, I've got three more rolls of very expensive film to shoot plus lots of notes to take or I don't get paid." She snatched up her camera and marched toward the east.

"Wait up, Beth. You shouldn't go off alone. I really don't understand how Ruth and Phil let you come here by yourself. You don't look both ways when you cross the street." Joshua grinned widely when he saw that his teasing words had their desired effect. Beth's precipitous flight stopped in midstep. She whirled around, glaring back at him.

"Very funny, Dr. Hunter, but contrary to your low opinion of my feet, I usually know where I'm putting them."

Her sore elbows and wrapped ankle gave her simultaneous twinges to belie that claim. Realizing how accident prone all her bandages made her look, Beth's expressive mouth quirked into an involuntary smile.

"OK, you're right. It's not good sense to work alone, especially here. The buddy system is safer."

"Well, I'd be happy to be your . . . buddy."

Beth felt her mind become mush when Joshua closed the distance between them and tilted her chin up to inspect her face.

She braced herself to do righteous, if reluctant, battle

with the lips that seemed poised to devour her own. After a long, tense moment, Joshua spoke of another kind of hunger.

"How about if I tag along with you and then we can come back here for a quick lunch? I've got some extra sandwiches with me. I'm sure we'll have time for you to take those photos and eat before Roger gets here to take me up to the crater. Maybe in the meantime, the device will start working right again and tell us enough so that I don't have to make the trip."

Joshua was surprisingly good at the stalking, waiting game Beth played to get close enough to photograph the wary creatures that had returned to live below the slopes of Mount St. Helens.

In addition to the elusive animals, there were static reminders of the violence that needed no stealth to study. Framing acres of blown-down trees in the small rectangle of her camera lens, Beth imagined she heard the echo of their silent scream of death. Taking picture after picture of the prostrate forest, she finally understood what force the volcano must have generated to fell such mature pines in a fraction of a second.

Her horror was relieved only when she found that new seedlings had taken root among the charred trees. But they were half a century away from their parents' former beauty.

However, nature was definitely making a return, even on the Plains of Abraham. Beth remembered from her research that the treeless, rock-strewn flats had never been a hospitable place to most life. Now, when the area was covered with dried, caked mud, she was delighted to find fireweed in the desolation. Seeds had evidently been blown there by the wind.

Regaining some height, Beth took a panoramic shot to the southeast, which encompassed the Plains and the

Muddy River—aptly named now that it was filled with the slides from several eruptions.

She added lupine and Cascade aster to her filmed collection of nature's returns. And when a spotted frog posed handsomely for her telephoto lens, Beth felt that she had earned her salary for the morning. Putting her camera into its case, she turned to the geologist standing a few feet away.

"Did you say something about sandwiches, Joshua? I'm famished."

"So what else is new?" he chuckled, obviously referring to last evening's dinner.

"Well, it's better than having to be afraid of every calorie you eat, breathe in, or rub on, like some people I know," Beth retorted.

"Meaning whom?" he challenged, looking down at his own flat stomach.

"Oh, not present company, I'm sure. I was thinking of my mother and sisters. They're all on perpetual diets. You won't have to worry about a pot belly—at least your father doesn't have one, and I'll bet you take after him," Beth opined.

"Maybe physically, but not in other ways, I hope," The bitterness in his voice astonished Beth.

"Joshua Hunter, what a nasty thing to say about your own father! I've just met him, but he struck me as being a very likable, decent man. He was sincerely upset when I hurt myself yesterday and . . ."

Beth had to forcibly restrain herself from pushing up her sleeves over the bandages, when that habitual gesture surfaced to signal her embarrassment.

"And *I* was boorish. I'm sorry about that—and a lot of other things," Joshua muttered an unexpected apology. "You're right, Dad does have a lot of redeeming qualities. My remark was just residual anger left over from an old problem. He's been a great help with the ongoing research these last eight years. And we've certainly come a long way since the decade in which we hardly talked to each other.''

''Research for eight years . . . you didn't talk for ten years . . . Joshua, just how old are you, anyway?'' Beth burst out before she could clamp a censor on her tongue.

''Looking forty right in the eye,'' he admitted, examining her face carefully for her reaction to that news. ''Must seem ancient to someone of your age. Twenty-three, twenty-four, right?''

''Thirty, next February.''

''Thirty? My God, when I first saw you, I thought you were sixteen.''

''Don't remind me. I get carded every single time I go to a place that serves alcoholic drinks. It's a great embarrassment to me.'' Beth grimaced and rolled her eyes heavenward, but she couldn't forget the disturbing statement Joshua had just made.

''Joshua, I've had my share of disagreements with my family, but do you really mean that you had a problem that would keep you apart from your father for that many years?'' The instant the question left her mouth, Beth realized how rude it was. ''Hey, I'm sorry. Don't answer that; it's absolutely none of my business. I'm not being nosy,'' she assured him.

Fortunately, he couldn't hear the sarcastic little voice in her head that wanted to know just whom she was kidding.

''Oh, it's not really a deep, dark secret. Nothing *I* have to be ashamed of,'' he told her. *And nothing compared to the things I do have on my conscience that I never want you to know about.* ''It all began with my father's work. You know that Dad's as much an oil man as a geologist?''

Beth nodded.

''Well, now he owns three companies that do exploration, refining, and research with petroleum. He sends teams around the globe to search for deep-lying deposits of oil and gas. However, when I was growing up, Dad was a free-lancer. Any firm that had his fee sent *him* all over the world. But he was never in one place long enough for them to let his family go along. My mother really wanted to go with him, too. She had this wild love of the unknown. She was always reading about faraway places. I guess before my brother and I came along, she was quite a daredevil. Sky-diving, hang gliding, spelunking. But Dad wouldn't let her go with him.

"So for years, Mom sat home, with the total responsibility of raising Carter and me. After a while, her anger at missing out on the life she really wanted finally got too much for her. She turned all her rage inward into a deep depression. It got to the point where Mom could hardly bring herself to leave the house anymore, or even choose what we were going to have for dinner."

Beth watched Joshua's finely cut features grow harder and more grim as he continued his disturbing story. She wanted to reach out, to smooth away the harsh line grooving between his dark eyebrows. She forcefully restrained herself while he plowed relentlessly through his bitter remembrances.

"My mother never let us tell Dad about her depressions. And somehow, she always managed to rally when he came home. He'd arrive, the conquering hero, with tales of faraway places and with gifts that made me the envy of the neighborhood.

"I worshipped him until I was fifteen. Then Mom got so bad, I finally figured out what he'd done to her." The darkness in his eyes compelled Beth to probe deeper.

"Why didn't she tell him? Why didn't she get help?"

"Hell, I don't know. Too proud, or maybe she loved him too much. She never said a harsh word about Dad. She was always telling us how much he loved us and how well he took care of us. Oh, I knew that he provided money, lots of it. But he was never there to help handle the problems or even to root for us at Little League.''

Beth watched him shake his head and laugh ironically, as if to deny that his father's benevolent neglect could still hurt after all these years. But he obviously still suffered with a wound that had not completely healed.

"I think the thing I hated most was that Mom made my brother and me keep a diary of what happened to us every day. We had to go through the entries whenever he showed up.''

"Why, that sounds like your father cared a lot about you and your brother.''

"Oh, you're right. It's obvious to an adult, but you wanted to know what started the rift." He raised a sardonic dark eyebrow at her. "I guess I just couldn't understand his wanderlust. When I was fifteen, I couldn't hide what I felt anymore; I stopped censoring my journal. The next time Dad read it, he quit and formed his own company. From then on, he took my mother and us everywhere he traveled. Of course, that was just when friends— girls—had become the most important thing to Carter and me. The two of us got dragged around the world, in and out of one school after another. I resented Dad for that, too.

"We also had horrendous fights over what he wanted to do with *my* life. It got so bad that I enlisted in the Army the day I turned eighteen.''

"Eighteen! You didn't go to college?" Beth broke in.

"Not then. Dad was hoppin' mad, which was why I did it. He'd already paid my first year's tuition and board at MIT. But I was bound and determined to show him I was independent of his money and his influence. Even if I got myself killed proving it.''

"He couldn't have bought your way into that school! You almost need an engraved invitation for them even to send you an application form. You must have impressed them on your own."

"Well, at the time, everything he wanted, I didn't. Even if I really did." Joshua grimaced, remembering his youthful foolishness.

"Did you ever get to MIT?"

"Yeah, after I got back from 'Nam. I have a degree from there in mechanical engineering," he admitted.

"Then what in the world are you doing teaching geology?"

Joshua ducked his head. Such a simple question . . . such a complex answer. He couldn't explain fully without telling her about Carol, so he gave Beth just a part of the truth. "I developed . . . an obsession with the subject. I went back to school and took a Ph.D. in it."

"Well, I'm glad you overcame your rebellion enough to do something that really interested you. I guess spending all those years back East explains why you don't have an obvious Texas accent, like your father," she observed.

"Oh, it's there, if you listen carefully, modified by a few Boston beans."

Beth's husky laughter seemed to warm the cool spring morning. And to Joshua's dismay, he knew that it also had begun to melt the ice in his heart.

"Joshua, how did you and your father reach the rapprochement you share now?"

He hesitated, his jaw working as he seemed to debate his next words. "It wasn't easy. Dad took a lot of guff from me until I let him back into my life, and that wasn't until . . ."

His voice trailed off and his gaze wandered to his clenched hands. In the silence that followed, Beth had the strangest feeling that this basically reticent man had told a relative stranger much more than she needed to know about his past, while revealing almost nothing about the present. Why he was constructing such a complicated smokescreen, she had no idea.

Beth found herself listening intently to his next words for some clue that would reveal what he was trying to hide.

"I really wanted to forgive him the day we buried my mother, six months after I enlisted. The Army let me fly back for the funeral. Dad was completely shattered. He had been out at a remote site when she suffered a heart attack. There was no decent hospital for hundreds of miles. Even though Mom had insisted on going to that primitive area, Dad still blamed himself. I should have ended it then, but I guess I was too immature, too guilty myself about running off and abandoning her.

"At the time, well, I was dumb enough to tell him that when I got married and had a family, *I'd* know how to take care of those who depended on me. I shouted at him that I would be there for every case of chicken pox, every broken bone, and each baby's first smile."

Tears stung Beth's eyes. She felt so bad for both father and son. Wanting to comfort Joshua, she rushed into speech without really thinking about what she was saying. "Joshua, I'm sure your wife and children are happy to have a man who feels like that."

Oh, damn, look at his face! He wasn't any taller, but Joshua loomed over her, a veritable giant in his anger.

"I mean, if you're married. That is, when you get married. Any future wife and children," she rapidly amended, trying to make up for her obvious gaffe.

"You're fishing, Beth. I have no wife . . . no child. Why would you think that I had a family?" he demanded. He should tell her that Carol never even had a chance to get pregnant . . . that her wonderful, loving husband prevented it by murdering her on their honeymoon! But he couldn't form those damning words. Instead he snarled,

"Like admitting that you're really not going to marry Price?" He grew absolutely still, awaiting her answer.

"You're not going to offer me an alternative, are you?"

The question had just popped out, and her large eyes pleaded with him to ignore her stupidity.

Joshua's body shuddered once. He appeared to be in a battle of conflicting desire. For a minute, Beth thought he was going to wrap her in his arms, but then he sighed and just let go of her hand.

"No, I'm not going to fool myself or mislead you. Beth, I'm not free now, and I may never be," he said gently, his eyes filled with sad regret.

She didn't know what she had expected, but it certainly wasn't that. Hurt and angry, Beth jumped up, yelling at him. "Not free? Talk about your classic case of 'Dog in the Manger!' Oh, you're free enough to kiss me, to think that you could seduce me away from Phil. You're free to let me make a damn fool of myself with you. To . . . to . . . oh, I don't even want to think about it!"

Joshua slowly rose from the rock, one hand reaching out toward her.

Turning away from him in disgust, Beth compulsively began picking up the remains of their lunch and stowing the litter away in her pockets.

"God, but you're selfish." She found herself unable to silence her contempt for the man. "You just think about yourself. Your wants and desires, no matter who gets hurt."

Grabbing her camera and backpack, Beth's flight was abruptly arrested by the small, harsh sound that tore out of Joshua's throat. When her eyes flew to his face, she found that he was staring at her. His features were twisted with so much suffering that she started to put her equipment down to go to him.

Then his pain turned to rage, and he roared back at her, "Don't pontificate at me, lady. Don't talk to me about desire. All I needed to do was touch you last night and you forgot every golden rule *you* were ever taught. You went wild!''

Closing the space between them before she could react, Joshua took her head in a viselike grip, burying his shaking fingers in the softness of her wind-blown hair.

''It would only take one kiss and you'd be begging me to take you here. Right here in this ash-covered graveyard.''

The golden rays in his irises pierced her soul, defying her to deny his statement. Beth made no attempt to refute him; he had spoken the simple truth of the matter. All she could do was silently damn him for saying it out loud, and damn herself for her weakness.

At that moment, the sun broke out of a chink in the clouds. A shaft of light haloed the area, illuminating Beth's face and hair. ''An angel in hell,'' Joshua whispered harshly. He released her head, holding his hands away from him as if the sun-tipped radiance of her curls and burned his fingers.

''Get out of here, Beth. Just get out of my sight.''

Neither one of them heard the low whump-whump of an approaching helicopter when his words pulled a stifled moan of agony from Beth's throat. Whirling around, she stomped back along the trail she had used to get to the mudflow. She prayed fervently that she would never see the miserable man again. She hoped that he would roast for eternity, slowly turning on a spit over some volcano's simmering caldera.

Joshua monitored Beth's precipitous flight. *Good job, Josh, you altruistic ass.* He mentally applauded the success of his loutish role-playing. *She really hates you now, buddy.* Well, that's what he had intended . . . to finish it, once and for all. It was far better this way than to face

Beth's revulsion at some future moment when she found out what he had done to Carol.

As a stinging whirlwind of dust swirled around him, Joshua's senses finally disengaged from his intense absorption with Beth to focus on the arrival of the company's smaller helicopter.

He made a half turn toward his equipment, but then Joshua felt compelled to take one last glimpse of Beth. Almost as if she had felt the weight of his gaze on her back, the small, retreating figure stumbled. His arms went up in an automatic gesture of aid, but Beth had already caught herself and trudged on. A deep sigh shuddered through Joshua's body; a wry smile twisted his mouth.

"Goodbye, you beautiful little klutz," he murmured.

Beth's heart couldn't keep up the frantic pace her anger had set for it. Ten minutes after leaving Joshua, she was forced to slow down her precipitous retreat. With the blood roaring in her ears she stopped to take a few deep breaths. Beth almost fell flat on her face when she looked up from the rugged trail she had been following and saw that there was a helicopter hovering just in front of her.

Staring at the machine through her protective goggles while it settled nearby, she saw a man gesturing to her from the open doorway. Joshua was frantically beckoning to her. Thinking that some disaster must have happened to her friends, she ran forward, ducking under the swirling blades.

"You really have a permit to go up to the crater?" Joshua shouted down at her.

Beth nodded dumbly, pointing to the zippered compartment on her jacket sleeve that held her identification.

"And you promise that you'll stay inside the helicopter?" he yelled.

It dawned on her that he was extending an invitation to

ride up to the crest of the volcano after all. Forcefully biting back the immediate refusal her pride demanded, the naturalist in Beth directed an affirmative bob of her head.

"Then get in here, woman. We don't have any time to waste."

Scrambling inside, Beth briefly wondered if *Reader's Digest* still solicited "My Most Unforgettable Character" essays. The quixotic Joshua Hunter would certainly qualify for hers.

SIX

"Strap yourself into the copilot's seat, Beth," Joshua directed after guiding her into the front section of the helicopter.

When she slid into her designated spot, the sandy-haired man at the controls held out his hand. "Glad to meet you, Beth. Roger Mulheny at your service."

"Stop charming the lady with your sophisticated patter, Mulheny, and get this crate up," Joshua said over the sound of the rotors.

Grinning at Beth, the pilot threw his employer a snappy salute and then quickly got the machine off the ground.

Beth had ridden in helicopters a dozen times before, but the sudden tilt of the horizon as Roger skimmed them up the side of the snow- and ash-dusted slope gave her a bad moment of disorientation. Then a few minutes into the flight, she couldn't help gasping out loud when the spray from a steaming waterfall covered the windows for a blinding second until the wipers whisked the moisture away.

They quickly rose above the hundred-foot-high cascade and Beth saw where the snow melt had gouged a deep erosion gully out of the pyroclastic debris on the mountain's flank. It seemed like only a moment later that they crested the jagged edge of the broken crater rim and entered into the caldera.

Beth had seen hundreds of pictures of the lava dome and she had read all the statistics about its size, but nothing prepared her for the sight of the venting structure below them.

It had been compared to San Francisco's TransAm Building in height and volume, but she would always think of it as a portal into hell.

Finally remembering to get her camera out of its case, Beth silently asked Roger's permission to open her side window to take unobstructed shots of the crater while they slowly circled in on their landing site. With his nod, she slid the glass open and began clicking away.

Twisting around in her seat, she noticed out of the corner of her eye that Joshua had just put on special heat-resistant boots and was about to fit a breathing mask to his face.

Without thinking, Beth snapped his picture just as Joshua grinned at her. She sighed inwardly, somehow relieved that she had captured that wicked dimple for posterity.

Later that afternoon, she would develop the film in her portable dark-room setup and receive a troubling jolt from the results. But right now, her attention was distracted when Roger called out to her.

"How about taking one of your brave and resourceful pilot, Beth?"

Laughing, she quickly complied with his request.

Her eyes immediately went back to Joshua. He was pushing a cloth-wrapped bundle toward the door. Without a word of farewell he leapt out of the machine onto the crater floor.

When he picked up his equipment and began trudging toward the lava dome five hundred yards away, Beth im-

mediately released her seat belt. She moved to the doorway and crouched in the opening to snap a picture of his
retreating form. She then took a dozen shots of the snow-
clad dome that towered over them, several plumes spewing
from steaming fumaroles. The feeling of being at the edge
of hell washed over her again.

His breath was a harsh sound within the breathing mask
when Joshua finally reached his goal, a bright-orange device with mirrors set into it at right angles. He quickly
checked the surfaces. Just as he had feared, he found that
the seals were cracked. They no longer protected the glass
from the acrid sulfuric emissions the dome periodically
exhaled. The exposed mirrors had been fogged by the
chemicals, resulting in the faulty data he had been getting.

Working quickly in the heavy air that smelled of rotten
eggs, he changed the old target for a new one. He repeated
the drill with two other devices before turning back to the
waiting helicopter.

Slogging through the ash toward the aircraft, a muffled
laugh escaped the mask covering his mouth. Beth had
stayed in the helicopter all right. There she was, her slight
body defying gravity while three-quarters of it precariously
hung out of the door.

She was snapping picture after picture, obviously not
wanting to miss this chance of a lifetime. That had been
the reason he changed his mind about bringing her up
here. The thought of her being denied this unique experience had somehow overridden his fear that she might hurt
herself.

When Beth finally noticed his approach, Joshua could
see a wave of trepidation cross her perfect features. As
she scuttled back toward her assigned seat, he felt an answering surge of remorse pass through him. He had never
wanted her to be afraid of him. He had only been concerned with her safety.

Joshua shook his head, wondering why the three most

important women in his life shared a reckless passion for adventure. Well, after failing miserably to keep his mother and then Carol safe from their obsession, he was determined that no harm would come to Beth while he was with her.

Pausing at the helicopter door, Joshua took off his mask and made himself look one last time at the distant scene framed by the smashed rim of the crater.

The worst of the volcano's devastating force had been funneled through that jagged notch. Somewhere out there—toward the northwest—ran the north fork of the Toutle River. After more than a decade, the tributary was still flushing away the wall of debris that had surged into it a few minutes after the mountain exploded.

Someday, maybe a thousand years from now, the river would finally clear itself of the ash and mud from Mount St. Helens. Joshua knew that sometime, from now until then, the earthly remains of Carol Hunter would be carried to her final resting place in the depths of the Pacific Ocean.

Beth felt the camp rock through three more minor tremors before the others in her documentary crew returned.

"Between that madman and this crazy mountain, I'm going to be a complete basket case by the time we leave here," she muttered while she paced the area following the first quake.

After completing his repair of the targets on the lava dome, Joshua had reentered the helicopter. He then quietly directed his pilot to drop Beth off near her base camp. Joshua wanted to go back to the mudflow site to try his experiment once more now that the targets had been repaired.

The short return flight had been made in virtual silence. It had been an anticlimax to Beth's disturbing day with Joshua Hunter. The episode had ended with a curt goodbye from him and a friendly wave of farewell from Roger Mulheny.

Unable to settle in one place when she reached her camp, Beth had decided to check the quality of some of the pictures she had taken. Setting up her portable darkroom in her tent, her hand hesitated and then settled on the next to last roll of film she had shot. The small metal canister contained the two photos of Joshua.

After completing the processing, she almost moaned with frustration when she hung up the contact sheet to dry and examined the tiny pictures with a magnifying glass. Most of them were just fine, but the ones she had taken of Joshua were hazed over with a strange blue light that blurred most of his features, including that wonderful dimpled smile.

The film must have gone bad, she decided. Then she noticed the frame she had taken of Roger sandwiched between the two shots of Joshua. She knew that she had snapped the pilot's picture after taking the first one of Joshua while he was still in the helicopter. Only after getting Roger's photo had she caught the second one of Joshua, trudging away toward the lava dome.

How strange. Roger's likeness was perfectly fine, but both snapshots of Joshua had that weird blue halo.

Shrugging away a creepy feeling that had the hair on the back of her neck stirring, Beth cleaned up her equipment and then went out into the camp once more.

Pacing restlessly around the perimeter of the clearing, she spotted the haphazard array of materials Phillip had begun organizing that morning. Beth decided to finish the job he had frantically started after the first earthquake hit them.

She packed up the nonessential equipment and supplies, readying them for quick transport to the rendezvous site where the government helicopter was scheduled to meet the crew the next afternoon.

Beth had just finished the chore when Ruth, Dana, and Phillip trudged in, tired and dirty. As she ran to make them a pot of coffee, Phil presented her with the carcass of a large jackrabbit he had already skinned and dressed out.

"Home is the hunter, Beth. Provisions for a ragout stew." He shoved the animal at her.

"Oh, Phil, I told you not to do this," she protested angrily.

"Don't be silly, meat's for eating. I got him with one shot; he didn't suffer. Still haven't lost the old skill. Dead-eye Price, they used to call me." Phil seemed too proud of himself to notice the disgust in Beth's eyes.

While she fumed, Beth washed off the meat, cutting it up and adding dehydrated vegetables to make an early supper for the others.

Too upset with both Joshua and Phil to eat, Beth just drank cup after bitter cup of steaming coffee until she suspected that she was just trying to rid herself of the lingering taste of Joshua's mouth on her tongue.

Groaning, she put down her mug and attempted to share the postdinner conversation with her coworkers.

"Dana, has Vancouver called about this activity?" Beth asked the radio operator when a light quake moved the ground again.

"I talked to them just before we got back to camp. They're still sure we're safe for the night, but they moved our pick-up time to noon tomorrow. They're expecting thunderstorms of possibly gale force in the early afternoon."

"Good thing you got all the equipment together, Beth. We'll start moving it out in the morning," Ruth put in. "Oh, hello!" She was looking past Beth. "Welcome, Josh. What brings you our way? Your father went back to your camp. He expected that you'd be there."

Beth moaned inaudibly as she heard his step behind her.

Was she never going to be rid of the galling presence of the man? Why was he dogging her? Hadn't he made it clear that they had no future together? Hadn't *she* done the same thing?

Unwillingly, she turned and saw that he was tired, weighed down by the equipment strapped ,o his back. Perversely, Beth found herself offering him a cup of hot coffee. However, she avoided his touch when he tried to give her fingers a grateful squeeze as he accepted the brew.

Never had eyes suited a personality more than the chameleon irises of Joshua Hunter, she thought, looking into their beautiful depths. Beth tried to read what was in his eyes. His earlier anger still lingered, but, incongruously, he seemed to be pleading with her to understand something he could never say out loud.

Before she sorted out the mixed message, Phil came over to put a possessive arm around her shoulders. His grip was so tight that Beth knew she couldn't shrug away from it without making a scene.

In the tense visual confrontation that ensued between the two men, Joshua appeared to concede Phil's claim on Beth by transferring his attention to the campsite.

"I'm glad you're packing up. My new calculations tell a very clear story. I'd say that old lady up there is about to put out a bit more than this ash."

Beth chastised herself. He hadn't come there *just* to harass her; he was concerned about the safety of the crew.

Phil's fingers on her shoulder tightened painfully. "When? How soon?" he demanded sharply of the geologist.

"Oh, we can get a night's sleep. In fact, I don't think it'll go for at least forty-eight hours. And don't worry, whatever comes out of the crater will be directed away from our camps. But why not play it safe? When are you scheduled for pickup?" he asked Ruth.

"Not until noon. The Forest Service 'copter is all booked up till then."

"That should be fine, but you could come out in my dad's chopper. It's at our call in Vancouver. We're leaving about nine tomorrow morning."

"No!" Beth's shouted protest surprised even herself. "We've got too much valuable equipment that we can't leave behind. We'll go out on schedule."

"Beth, Dad's got two 'copters over at the airport. The other one is a hauling variety," Joshua said, trying to reason with her. "It has enough room for all of us, plus our gear. Phil and I can start bringing it to my camp right now. We can make as many trips as necessary. You can pitch your tents and sleep at our site tonight."

His slightly raised eyebrow challenged Beth. She valiantly fought to control the blush that threatened to engulf her neck and face.

"Oh, by the way, you lost your lens cap this afternoon, Beth." He held out the innocuous black circle.

Beth looked at it as if she had no inkling of its function or connection to herself. Then she realized that the blasted man was still determined to undermine what he thought was her continuing relationship with Phillip. Beth couldn't understand why. He had made it painfully clear that he didn't want her for himself.

Extending a shaking hand for the protective disc, Beth snatched it away from his long fingers. She forcefully conveyed her awareness of his treacherous tactic with the amber-edged daggers she directed at his wickedly innocent eyes.

The deep-dimpled smile he used for a shield deflected her thrust. It was a defense that seemed designed to dissolve every joint in her body and reduce her to a quivering mass of protoplasm on the ash-covered earth.

Beth shrank back from the devastating onslaught, moving closer to the dubious protection of Phil's arm. She abruptly wondered when *that* man would ask the obvious questions and fly into one of his jealous rages. Surprisingly, although Phil had heard the dialogue and watched the lens cap change hands, he totally ignored the implications.

"Well, what are we waiting for?" he asked instead. "Let's pack it up." His voice was abnormally high as he turned, trying to decide which pile to tackle first.

"Yes, I think Phil's right, too," Ruth spoke up. "Dana, why don't you take the radio and sound equipment with the guys right now? Then we'll be sure that the most valuable stuff gets there. Beth and I will break down the tents and pack the rest here for the second trip."

Wondering just how it had happened, Beth found herself outvoted. She was going to have to endure the night and part of the next day near the irritating source of her open wounds.

When the others had loaded up with as much as they could carry and left camp, Ruth walked over to her. "Honey, I want to talk to you," she said, her voice soft with concern. Beth had no doubt of the subject Ruth wanted to discuss.

"I don't care to talk about him," she protested.

"Which one, Beth?" Ruth chided gently.

"Oh, Ruth . . . look, I've discussed things with Phil. I've told him several times that I am not serious about him. He refuses to believe me. Luckily, now he's preoccupied with this threat of volcanic activity, so I'm just going to keep out of his way until we leave. When we go back to Los Angeles, I'm sure he'll be more reasonable. OK?"

"And what about Joshua? Beth, you've been searching for a long time. Don't turn your back on the man just because he's got problems. It won't be easy, but the way the electricity arcs between you two . . . well, isn't *that* what you've been waiting for?"

"Waiting for Joshua? I don't believe you, Ruth. He doesn't have any interest in me and I have none in him!"

Beth reddened when her boss almost choked on the laughter that declaration instigated.

"Well, he doesn't!" Beth insisted. Then honesty forced her to amend that statement. "All right, I'm attracted to him. But Ruth, I practically threw myself at Joshua this afternoon—verbally, at least—and he told me that he wasn't free. Just like you said yesterday, he's all tied up, somehow. Do you know what he means? You must; you spent hours with his father last night and today."

"He's not married, honey. He's not the type to lead you on, if that's what you're worried about."

"Oh, I know he's not married," Beth acknowledged in measured tones. "Is he engaged . . . living with someone . . . going steady . . . holding hands? Gay? No, forget about that one; no way!" she laughed ruefully. "For God sakes, Ruth, what does 'not free' mean?"

"I can't tell you," her friend confessed.

"What?" Beth all but shouted.

"I mean, I have some ideas, but that's it." Ruth tried to explain. "You could ask Stuart, but I don't think he'll tell you anything more than he told me . . . just that Josh isn't married. I know Stuart's tickled pink that Josh is obviously crazy about you. However, he said that he's given his pledge not to talk to us about the situation. Stu feels he has to prove something to his son, in order to regain his trust. Beth . . . just give him a chance."

"Ruth," she said with great dignity, "he just doesn't want me, and you can't make someone love you. I understand that very well; I've had a lifetime of experience with that little fact of human nature."

When Ruth couldn't counter that statement, Beth turned and walked over to the nearest tent. She began stuffing it into its covering. Her mind was in a turmoil. One part of her snatched at the idea Ruth had proposed, of following the lightning bolt of her emotions to earth and waiting to see if anything really could develop between her and Joshua.

The thought of him—his face, those eyes, that exciting body—created a heart-wrenching thrill every time she conjured up his image.

She couldn't forget the force of his kisses or the hot trail his hands left whenever he touched any part of her body. And although she had fought admitting it, there was a lot more to the attraction than his perfect physique and its effect on her. He was intelligent and humorous and talented . . .

Not that it mattered. While she went from tent to tent, breaking down each shelter and packing it away, Beth kept telling herself that the man and his attributes had no bearing on her life; her path and Joshua's had no common ground. Yet, perversely, she still pondered his statement that he wasn't free.

He had meant that he wasn't free to love her—just to *make* love to her. Yet, without love, there could be no true relationship between man and woman, nothing beyond the lustful coupling of needful bodies.

It hadn't been love last night, or this morning. It had been want, hers and his; they had physically needed each other. But what about all the rest she had to offer—everything else she had learned and squirreled away to amaze and amuse the man she had hoped to love one day? She had so much to give, but she wanted to receive as much in return.

When she first met him, Beth had thought she and Phil might be able to provide each other with that totality. However, her physical reaction to Joshua devastatingly proved how blind she had been. Beth had to be honest with herself. Even if she spent the next hundred years with Phil, he could never satisfy her emotional needs. Just a few moments in Joshua's arms had shown her what passion she had bottled up inside her. She had been waiting for him and no one else.

It was ironic. Together, Phil and Joshua were the perfect man for her; separately, both were lacking. Not that she had a choice. She could never love Phil as a husband . . . and Joshua? Well, Joshua had said that he wasn't free.

Beth had come full circle and was still wrestling with her twisting, turning thoughts when Phil, Dana, and the Hunters came into the camp.

Ruth beamed at Stuart when she saw him. She went to him with outstretched hands. He grabbed them and they walked around the camp, whispering like co-conspirators in a delicious secret.

At first, Beth thought they might be talking about Joshua and herself. Then, observing their faces, it became clear that they were delighted with each other. A whole lot had transpired between them since last evening.

Catching Beth watching his father and her friend, and then tossing him a worried glance, Joshua found himself responding with a warm smile for her. He could see the fight she waged within herself not to send one back to him. It was obvious that she didn't want anything more to do with him. Beth had barely looked his way, let alone talked to him, since he had given back that lens cap.

But in the next second his heart did a strange little two-step when Beth offered him one of her generous, if ironic, grins. It said that even if things were impossible for the two of them, she was glad that he could accept the love that had sprung up between Ruth and Stuart.

Looking at the tall man gazing at her from across the campsite, Beth sighed deeply at the thought of what might have been. At least Joshua's unclouded smile told her that the breach between father and son had finally been healed. Joshua had really forgiven Stuart and wished him well. Beth liked to think that their discussion about his traumatic childhood had helped.

Somehow, Joshua's good humor lifted her out of the introspective funk. While there could be nothing between them except a truce, Beth accepted that much with a little nod of her head.

With all of them working, the dismantling of the camp only took half an hour. It appeared that the six people, heavily loaded, could just manage hauling the remainder in one trip. With dusk approaching, they started out for the Hunter compound.

Thanking the heavens for small favors, Beth was relieved when Joshua chose to accompany his father on the journey. However, the penalty for that little victory was that Phillip Price now walked next to her, trying to match her faltering stride. Her bandaged foot throbbed under the burden she carried, and the others quickly outdistanced her hobble.

"What's wrong, Beth?"

"Oh, I twisted my ankle last night. It's not bad, but I'll have to go slowly. Why don't you go on ahead, Phil?"

"No way. This'll give us some privacy. I feel like I've been sharing you with the combined staff of public television and the U.S. Geologic Survey," he complained.

In spite of herself, Beth couldn't help laughing at his pained expression.

"I'll be glad when it's just the two of us, honey. All we need is each other. We can forget about the rest of the world."

The sudden fervor in his voice shocked her, and she knew that she had to end this once and for all.

"Phil, I . . . I want you to understand that as much as I like you, I don't want to marry you."

He stopped walking and turned toward her; his blue gaze abruptly lost any hint of humor.

"Oh, I think I *understand* what you're saying. I may have a lot of faults, but being stupid isn't one of them.

You've found the perfect excuse for dumping me. A wealthy geologist, right? You think I didn't figure out that you spent the day working alongside him? What I want to know is, just what was it that you two worked on—and on which side!"

"Phillip!" Beth gasped, shocked by his crude statement. "Oh, Phil, he has nothing to do with this. It was over between you and me even before we arrived on the mountain. You must acknowledge that. In fact, a serious relationship never really got started. Admit that we're just not right for each other, that it would never work between us."

She said it as bluntly as she could, knowing that a clean break would leave the least scarring on either of them.

"Yeah, you're right, it won't work. No guy wants an iceberg for a wife. You just better pray that your new friend doesn't find out how frigid you are before you've hooked him, baby."

Phil stalked away from her. His hand sliced through the deepening gloom with a final, dismissive gesture and his long legs soon outdistanced Beth. Yet, his cruel words seemed to rebound from the boulders edging the trail.

Beth wanted to shout after him that his taunt was untrue, but he had already disappeared. Well, let him save his pride, she decided before trudging after him, her misery weighing her down far more than the heavy load she carried.

SEVEN

The last glow of sunset was ebbing out of the sky when Beth rounded the rock outpost of the Hunter camp. She had gotten there five minutes after everyone else, but no one noticed her late arrival.

The others were all clustered around the limp form of Stuart Hunter, who was slumped on a camp chair. It appeared that Joshua had just stripped the heavy equipment from his father's back and was slipping a pill into his mouth.

"Put this under your tongue, Dad, and take a few deep breaths. You'll be all right in a minute," he assured him.

Beth laid down her burden and joined the worried circle, putting a comforting hand on Ruth's shoulder. Her friend stood there with a calm face, but she was clenching and unclenching her hands behind her back.

The lantern on the camp table documented Stuart's return of color; the ashen-gray of his face gave way to a more normal tan. Beth could see his purple lips redden when the nitroglycerine dilated his coronary arteries, promoting the free flow of blood again.

Relief surged through Beth when she saw Joshua relax. She gave Ruth's shoulder an encouraging squeeze.

"Well, Dad, time we all turned in. We've got an early date with your chopper in the morning."

"Right, son . . . you're right. Good night, everybody." He managed to sound jaunty, although Beth could see how shaky he was when he tried to get up.

Trying to appear nonchalant, Joshua bent to give his father a hand and then supported him over to the large tent. Ruth followed along, helping to cover Stuart with a blanket after his son deposited him on a bunk.

Somehow feeling that she was intruding, Beth pulled her attention away from the scene and began setting up her own shelter. When Phil and Dana did the same, Phillip made a great show of putting his tent at the opposite end of the camp, very near to Dana's.

Beth sighed. Maybe she could talk to Phil when his anger with her had cooled. It would be nice to retain his friendship. She had done that with almost every other man she had dated. They called her all the time just to chat. Nevertheless, this situation was very different, she had to admit. Shaking her head, Beth suspected that Phil probably would never want to talk to her again.

Ruth's return drew Beth out of her musings. Picking up her bedroll, the older woman smiled at her. "I'm going to help keep a watch on Stu. See you in the morning."

" 'Night, Ruth. Call me if you need anything."

Inside the main tent, Joshua looked up when Ruth reentered. "Why don't you take the other cot," he offered when he saw that she meant to unroll her sleeping bag on the canvas floor.

"Oh, that's not necessary. I'll be comfortable enough down here." She sank onto the thick material. "I won't be sleeping much, anyway." Ruth looked at Stuart

Hunter, who was fast asleep thanks to the mild sedative Joshua had administered.

"I don't think I'll be getting much rest, either," Joshua admitted. His eyes were drawn of their own accord through the raised tent flap to the slight figure gracefully moving around the cook stove.

"Josh, it's none of my business . . . No, damn it, it *is* my business. Beth is my friend, my best friend. I don't want to see her hurt any more than she already has been."

"Ruth, I don't want to hurt her any more, either . . ." Joshua began.

"No, I don't mean whatever has passed between you two. I'm talking about the years of misery she's suffered with unrequited love."

"Unrequited love? Is she involved with someone else . . . someone who's used her? Some married jerk who's led her on . . ."

"Joshua, stop. Beth has never been seriously involved with anybody. It's her family I'm talking about—her parents and her sisters. Beth's mother and father have always treated her like a mistake, an unwanted inconvenience. She was an honor student in high school, but when she refused to study fine arts, they wouldn't pay for her education, or even her room and board. They more or less disowned her. Oh, she got scholarships, but Beth still had to work two jobs to keep herself in school. That's why she just got her doctorate last semester.

"Even then her parents couldn't be bothered with attending her graduation ceremony. Neither did her sisters— Flossy, Popsy, or Bossy. Would you believe that those big blond cows tried their best for years to convince Beth that she was an unattractive dwarf?"

"My God! Beth couldn't really think that. Why, she's the most—"

"Yes, I know," Ruth interrupted softly, a suspicious glaze of moisture in her green eyes. "By now Beth should have figured out for herself that nobody else sees her as anything but beautiful. But deep inside, I think she still has doubts. That's why I'm telling you this, Josh. A blind person would know how you feel about each other. So please don't hurt her. I don't think she would ever be the same if *you* let her down."

"I don't intend to, Ruth." *Because after tomorrow, I'll never see her again,* Joshua vowed silently.

Not feeling sleepy yet, Beth went to the camp stove to make some fresh coffee. Its rich aroma had just begun to penetrate the sulfur-laced air when Joshua came out of his father's tent and slowly trudged toward her.

"How is he?" Beth handed the tall man a cup of the hot brew.

"The damned fool! Oh, he'll be all right. He was just trying to impress Ruth, carrying all that stuff. His heartbeat is strong and steady now. He'll be fine by morning if he doesn't try to impress her any more tonight."

Beth suppressed a giggle, equally motivated by relief and amusement over Joshua's pun.

"Why don't you get some rest, too, Beth?"

"Oh, I'm not quite zonked out yet. Besides, I want to spell you off," she protested. "You must be exhausted."

He nodded, stretching tired muscles, then folding his long body into the chair next to her.

"How are your wounds, by the way?" He reached over and gently stripped the worn bandages she had put on in the morning. "Looks good," he observed, examining her upturned elbows. "No infection, and scabs are forming. Try not to knock them off and I doubt that you'll have any scars."

His eyes held hers for an expectant second. Long fingers slid down her arms, leaving ten living trails of fire on her skin.

Perhaps no physical scars, she thought to herself when he seized her hands, ignoring her bemused protests.

Out of the corner of her eye, Beth saw Phil come out of his tent. She jerked her hands out of Joshua's grip, but not before Phillip observed the tableau in the lantern's light and then retreated inside.

Beth rose, intending to go to her tent, but Joshua was instantly in front of her, trapping her, holding her close to his broad chest. She could feel the strong, steady beat of his heart against her ear, which he pressed to the roughness of his shirt.

"Why don't you release him, Beth? Let him off the hook."

"Hook?" she groaned softly. When he ran his large hands over her captured form, she felt the biting tug of the set Joshua had ensnared her with dig deeper into her own body.

She tensed with fearful expectation. Afraid of him . . . more afraid of herself. Then he just sighed, giving her soft curls a last caress before he released her from his bondage.

"Go to bed, Beth. You look wiped out. I'll wake you if I need your help, I promise."

Beth didn't require any more encouragement. She fled to her tent. As it had done the previous evening, her mind closed down almost instantaneously. It knew that she needed the respite to sort out the dilemma that her life had become.

In the earliest part of the morning, Beth was shaken awake. Her strange, disturbing dreams of a tall, blond woman trying to tell her something important were replaced by a very real nightmare. Sharp retorts boomed repeatedly from the crest of the volcano. Fighting out of her sleeping bag, she waded into a curtain of ash that increased in density by the minute.

Ruth and the Hunters rushed from the main tent, but feeling the thick grit in the air, Joshua pushed the older couple inside again.

"Stay with Dad," Beth heard him direct Ruth. "There's nothing the two of you can do out here."

The three younger people converged on Joshua in an agitated circle; three sets of eyes automatically turned toward him when he casually sat on an edge of the camp table to talk with them. His deep voice and sturdy body were a calm epicenter in the chaos that swirled around the group. With several softly spoken sentences, he took charge.

"Let's fold up this place, folks. First, Beth, get some pillowcases and cut us face masks. If this ash gets thicker, we'll have to cover our noses with wet material. I'll contact Dad's pilot in Vancouver and get the big chopper on its way. Phil, why don't you and Dana begin making a triage of the equipment? I'll help you after I make that call."

The blond man ignored the request to begin pacing in front of the group like a cornered beast. When Beth placed a worried hand on his arm, he violently shrugged it away, and then he challenged Joshua.

"When do you think that mountain's going to blow, Hunter?" he demanded.

"According to my calculations, it won't be today. Those ventings of steam and ash are a good sign, Phil. It helps reduce the pressure and prevent a big one," he assured the frantic man.

"I want to know the truth, Hunter. What are our chances? Don't patronize me with any guff; that's for weaklings and women." He gripped Joshua's upper arm with white knuckles.

"Like I said, Phil," Joshua repeated evenly, "I really don't think we have a thing to worry about. I'll have the pilot start out at full light. Let me make that call and we'll be out of here by nine or so." He pried the man's rigid fingers off his arm.

"Why don't you help Dana move the heavier equipment to the pad?" he instructed Phillip again. "Beth, could you also make us some breakfast?" He looked up at the fall of ash. "Get those masks done before you start the food, though," he advised as he walked toward the communications equipment.

When Joshua finished talking to Roger, he helped Phil move some of the heaviest apparatus. Leaving the nervous man with the calming task of arranging the materials, Joshua came back to where Beth had put together a hasty breakfast.

"Roger will be here by nine-thirty. There's a heavy storm front heading this way and we'll have to hustle the loading." Joshua helped her dish out bowls of hot oatmeal and then went to call the others for the meal.

Beth was pouring coffee when her boss emerged from the large tent. "Hi, Ruth. How's Stu doing now?" she asked in a low voice.

"Oh, he's fine, Beth, he really is just fine. Stu has to remember that he isn't twenty-five, which is hard for a man like him to admit. Once we're out of here, I don't think there'll be any more problems." Ruth smiled. Her eyes looked tired, but happier than Beth had ever seen them before.

"I'll take him some breakfast, Josh, and I'll keep him quiet while you get things ready out here," she informed his son on her way back to the recovering man.

Beth's eyes followed her to just beyond the Hunter tent where Dana was arguing with Phil. She plucked at his sleeve when he vehemently shook his head, obviously refusing to join them for food. As he turned to stack some camping supplies, Phil noticed that Beth was watching him. He threw the materials down, grabbing Dana by the hand. Slinging a possessive arm around the tall girl, he almost dragged her to the table, glaring defiantly at Beth.

Phillip gulped down three cups of hot coffee in rapid succession, but didn't seem to have an appetite for food.

"It might be a long time until lunch, Phil. At least have a piece of toast," Beth urged.

"I'm really not hungry, sweetheart." When Phil's automatic words penetrated his mind, he banged the mug down and stomped over to the smaller tents where he began taking them apart.

"Beth, please talk to him," Dana said in an urgent whisper. "I'm worried about all the stress he's under. But he won't listen to anything I say."

This was the opening Beth needed. She was determined to convince Phil that Dana was the woman who truly loved him. Perhaps she could also salvage their friendship. Putting down her dish, she gave Dana a warm smile before going over to help Phil with his self-imposed task.

"I'll sure be glad to leave here and get a hot shower. This ash is making my skin itch . . ." she began.

He just grunted, not cooperating at all. Phil cast a worried eye to the crater of the volcano, now covered with clouds of rapidly moving, swirling vapor.

"Looks like that weather cell Vancouver warned us about has arrived," Beth tried again. "Phil . . . I know this isn't a very good time, but I'd really liked to—"

"Damn it, Beth, just give up," he finally shouted at her. "I'm not about to join your entourage of ex-boyfriends. Don't expect any pathetic phone calls from me!"

Halfway across the camp, Dana and Joshua both looked over, their faces mirroring concern.

"We're finished; make it a clean break." Phil's voice lowered to an angry hiss. "Go work on Hunter, maybe he has what you need. Maybe being crazy in love with you isn't what you want from a man. You probably need a guy who can take you or leave you and treats you rotten. Oh, hell . . . just get away from me."

With his feature contorted by reined-in violence, Phil snarled an oath and swung on Beth.

Joshua had already taken half a dozen steps toward the pair when he saw Price abort the gesture just a scant inch away from Beth's shoulder. Even though he never touched her, Beth staggered back a little, but she quickly regained her balance.

While Joshua hesitated a second, debating what to do next, Phil cursed again and then turned away from Beth. He began stuffing the slick material of Dana's shelter into its cover.

With pride and anger taking over from guilt and misery, Beth whirled on her heel and stomped over to clean up the remains of breakfast. She assiduously avoided looking at the pair who helped her in tactful silence, but out of the corner of her eye, she saw the ambivalent little smile that came and went on Dana's lips.

Joshua's expression was carefully blank; no hint of his thoughts was evident on his ruggedly handsome face. However, Beth wondered about the agitated pulse that beat under his jaw and the light film of perspiration sheening his forehead.

For the next hour, they somehow sublimated the tensions twanging between them into the effort needed to break down of the campsite. Finally, after sorting and packing everything, the weary group sat near the landing pad. They were all clad in waterproof slickers that helped protect them from the fall of ash and the spattering of infrequent raindrops.

Two more quakes shook the ground as nine-thirty neared. By then, the cinders were thick enough for Joshua to insist that his father put on a wet mask. He didn't like how Stuart Hunter's breathing had become hoarse and labored.

Nine-thirty passed with no sign of the rescue craft and with ever-increasing winds.

Breaking the oppressive silence, Ruth joked with Stuart. "You know, if we had waited for the government copter, we'd have needed snowshoes to get through this gunk."

The two older people gripped hands and Ruth kept a light banter going, obviously trying to soothe the heavily breathing man.

"What's keeping that chopper?" Phil jumped up, sending plumes of the gathering ash flying out in all directions. Stuart started coughing and hacking, prompting Beth to give him a freshly moistened face mask and help him change from the old one.

Seeing the frantic, intense look on Phil's face, Joshua casually placed himself between the blond man and the rest of the group.

"Hey, Phil, I'll bet you recognize Dad's chopper the minute it gets here. It might be the same model you flew in 'Nam. He got it from government surplus a few years ago. A real workhorse; it lifts loads you wouldn't believe. Hell, what am I telling *you* this for." He slapped his forehead with an ironic palm. "You know their capabilities, of course."

Joshua went on talking to the pacing man, trying to calm him with good-natured reminiscences of some of the better things he recalled about the war.

". . . and did you ever meet my dad's pilot, Roger Mulheny? He flew supply, too. Now there's a guy who—"

"Shut up, Hunter. Just shut your mouth. Don't try to be *my* buddy. You know what you've done here. What's the secret? How did you melt the Ice Maiden? Have to give you that. I can see that you finally got her going," he challenged.

"Quiet, Price. Keep your own mouth closed. Don't say anything else," Joshua ordered.

"What are you going to do about it, try and deck me? I've had all the same training, pal. Hah! Well, you're welcome to her. Wait till you try to get her to bed. Boy, will you be surprised."

Phil turned away in disgust, but Joshua pulled the angry-eyed man around by the shoulder, capturing the fist that Phil threw at him with his other hand, forcing it into a position high over his dark head. Stuart started to rise before either man could pull loose from the grip that clamped their fingers together. But Ruth held him back while Dana ran over to the struggling men.

Dana grabbed Phillip around the waist, and with surprising strength, dragged him away from Joshua before any damage was done—physically.

Watching the ugly scene, Beth felt a sudden numbing paralysis that seemed to nail her boots to the pumice-covered ground. She was tempted to close her eyes to their storm-filled faces and shut her ears to the appalling words.

As Phillip shook off Dana's restraining hold, he seemed ready to lunge at Joshua again. But on the edge of renewed aggression, he stopped and stood stock-still.

"Listen . . . listen!" he shouted. His rage forgotten, he responded to the faint throb in the air. The vibration increased until the hope-filled beat pulsed in every ear.

Searching his pockets for a match, Joshua ran to fire the four flares he had stuck into the ground around the perimeter of the landing area. They lit the ash-induced gloom with their reddish, actinic glow. Appearing out of the mists a few seconds later, the helicopter zeroed in on their brilliance.

"Everybody, protect your faces!" Joshua warned, as the fine ash was whipped into a cyclonic frenzy by the blades of the hovering craft.

After an eternity of waiting, the motion ended and the large doors were opened by the grinning pilot.

"Boy, am I glad to be down! That wind is sure gusting. The mountain's shielding us some here, but a few hundred feet south, it's up to thirty-five knots." Roger shook his head in disbelief. "We haven't got much time, folks, so let's get this stuff loaded and get out of here. I'm more worried about the storm than that old biddy of a volcano up there."

The short, sandy-haired man jumped down to help with the evacuation.

"Roger, get my dad in first," Joshua directed. "He's having trouble breathing from the ash. By the way, everyone, this is Roger Mulheny."

"Hello to all. Nice to see you again, Beth," he replied cheerfully. "Say, Mr. Hunter, I sure do like your mask; looks like you're ready to perform brain surgery."

Joking with his boss, Roger boosted him up into the front of the machine. Ruth hopped in and sat with Stuart.

The next half hour passed in a blur of hauling and stowing the invaluable possessions of both teams into the wide cargo hold that filled all too rapidly.

"We don't need to take all this junk," Phil protested when they handed up the PBS tents and sleeping bags. "It'll weigh us down too much. We'll never get off the ground," he predicted, his voice getting louder and more desperate as the equipment was passed up.

"Phil, we've got plenty of power to spare," Stuart explained. His face was now free of the mask and he was breathing more normally.

"We have to save what we can of the camping gear," Ruth agreed. "We're obligated to return it. Public Television just doesn't have the money for replacements, Phillip."

"But it could shift in this turbulence. Don't put it in here with us," the blond man pleaded.

Amid the arguments, the first of a series of rapidly escalating tremors went unnoticed. By the time the severity and length of the event was recognized, the camp and the loaded helicopter were shaking with unusual vibrations.

"Get in!" Phil screamed hysterically. "Forget the rest, let's get the hell out of here." He jumped into the cargo hold, pulling Dana along with him. He held out his hand for Beth, but as she reached for it, she abruptly pulled back, shrieking, "My camera, I forgot my camera!"

She turned and raced to the spot outside the landing area where she had left it. Grabbing the Nikon, she couldn't resist taking shots of the copter glowing eerily in the red flare light. It quivered like a gigantic dragonfly out of the dim reaches of the Mesozoic past.

Totally involved with capturing the scene, Beth jumped when she heard Joshua's approving chuckle next to her. "Enough is enough, Dr. Cristie. Let's get the hell off this mountain," he advised, grabbing her hand.

Perhaps it was seeing the two of them running together, heads thrown back in shared amusement, that unhinged Phil's strained nerves. Feelings of frustration and hatred pushed reason from his eyes. He pulled his target pistol from his jacket and menaced the rest of the astonished crew.

"Get this crate up. Nothing else gets loaded. You can come back for the rest of this junk and those two after I'm safe. If you don't lift off right now, Mulheny, I'll push you out and fly it myself." He swiveled his body around to keep his eye on the others.

"Wait, Phil," Joshua shouted into the machine. "At least take Beth with you. She'll hardly add a hundred pounds to your load. You know you've got power to spare. Think, man!" Joshua yelled, trying to push Beth into the doorway. "Roger, throw me the extra radio, I'll wait here until you get back."

The fear in Beth's wide eyes seemed to penetrate Phil's own terror. With a body-shaking sigh, he relented and reached out his hand for her. Instinctively, she thought of her camera and passed that valuable apparatus up first. Phil ripped the Nikon out of her slender fingers, but as another quake hit, he bellowed in renewed panic and pushed her back into Joshua's arms.

"Get away from the wash, Hunter. Take her with you. You two hit it off so well, keep each other company. But I'm getting out of here in one piece, not like what happened to me in 'Nam." Phil motioned for Dana to close the door. She hesitated, looking between the two adversaries.

Joshua tried to reason with Phil again. "OK, let's push out a hundred pounds of equipment." When he attempted to lift Beth up, the stinging breeze of a bullet zinged past his ear. The near miss came within an inch of his head.

Beth launched herself back into Joshua's arms, causing them to roll out of the sight line of the crazed man. When Joshua tried to get up again, she screamed, "No, he's a crack shot, he'll kill you! We can be out of here in another hour and a half. Let them go. Stuart has to get out of this ash," she pleaded.

Shaking off her restraining hands, Joshua stood up slowly. He walked back into the range of the gun leveled at him. "At least give us that radio, Price. We have to keep in contact." His voice was steady, his words controlled.

Phil hesitated. "OK, toss it out, but no tricks."

Joshua nodded to Roger when the ambivalent man looked at him questioningly. "Do as he says. Just toss it down to me. Get my dad and the others back, Roger. I'll see you on the next trip. Good luck. So long, Dad." He waved to his father, who had a gray, sick look on his face.

Stuart tried to rise, but Ruth held him down.

"It'll be all right, Beth," she called. "Just stick with Josh . . ." Her voice was abruptly cut off by the silencing thickness of the metal door slamming shut.

_____ EIGHT _____

As the helicopter gunned away, Joshua pulled Beth from
the ash-filled blade wash, out of the glowing circle of
flares that had seemed like such a welcoming sign of safety
just a few minutes before.

While the stinging particles settled around them, Beth
buried her face on Joshua's chest, feeling shudder after
shudder of fear and tension be absorbed by that strong,
hard expanse. With their arms encircling each other, Beth
momentarily imagined that they were alone in the universe
and were the only life of any importance.

When the last trembling had abated, Joshua tilted up
her chin and looked at her tear-stained face.

"Tryouts for Ringling Brothers' Clown Corps aren't
until next week, Ms. Cristie." With a wide grin, he fished
for a handkerchief in his back pocket and used the remaining tears on her cheeks to wipe away streaks of
grime.

Attempting to lighten the despair that still weighed
down her features, Joshua summed up the situation.
"Well, Beth, now we know what Phil really wanted from

you all along. It wasn't marriage . . . he just coveted your Nikon.''

Somehow Beth didn't flare in anger at the tasteless absurdity of his declaration. Instead, she found her mouth curling into an involuntary grin.

His hearty chuckle provoked slightly hysterical giggles from her. Their mirth grew to an uncontrolled intensity until the pair had to prop each other up to keep from doubling over in the pain of that humorous release.

When Beth's helpless laughter turned into hiccoughs, Joshua lifted her arms high over her head, claiming it was an ancient Hindu remedy that had been given to him by a guru from Tibet.

After the spasms subsided, he took her captured hands and placed them around his neck. Before she could protest, Joshua pulled Beth's head to his chest again, stroking her soft hair until she conquered her jittery nerves and was able to raise sober eyes to meet his. They looked at each other for frozen seconds, each searching for something they were loath to name . . . neither sure what they would do if they found it.

The jagged breath Beth finally took seemed to end Joshua's paralysis, and his mouth slowly lowered toward hers. In the beginning, his kiss was simply a recognition that they had survived a dangerous moment. Then the light brush on her lips ignited Beth and she put her total longing for the man into returning his kiss.

Joshua shuddered at her intensity. With a hoarse groan of utter helplessness, he brought his own pent-up need to the passion that grew between them.

His mouth found hers again, while his hands roamed over her hips. He lifted her up to him, molding her slight form to his lean body and rising male strength, just like he had done on the night they had danced together.

Instead of being shocked and afraid this time, Beth moved against him, responding with a rhythm buried deep in her collective unconscious; a gift from generations of lovers that had led up to her conception and that now guided her instinctive movements.

Joshua pulled his head back at last, tearing his mouth from hers with a harsh sound. His breathing was labored in the thick atmosphere of ash and desire.

"Beth, what are you doing to me? You make me forget what I must remember. You make me want to wrap my body around yours and take you . . . right here, right now. I want to bury myself in you so deeply that you'll never be free of me." He held on to both sides of her face, torment in his eyes.

"But I can't, sweetheart. I can't do what I want to do and then not be able to give you all the rest you deserve. Try to understand, darling. I'm not fit to be your lover or anything else." He closed his eyes tightly, unable to bear looking at her any longer.

A strangled cry was torn from Beth's throat. He had done it again! Joshua had stirred her body and played with her emotions. Yet, the obvious pain he was in kept her from hitting out at him, physically or verbally. Instead, she probed for the source of his anguish, trying to understand it, to find some way to assuage the hurt he had buried within himself.

"What is it, Joshua, what's done this to you?" she asked in agony.

Joshua shook his head. "I can't even talk to you about it, Beth. It goes too deep and hurts so much, I just can't get it out. Besides, you'd despise me if I did."

When he buried his face on her breast, Beth couldn't help caressing the back of his neck and massaging the tension that had tied his shoulder muscles into tight steel cables.

"Did something horrible happen in Vietnam?" It was the only thing she could imagine that would torment him so much.

His muffled laugh was harsh. "Something horrible happened there every day, Beth. But don't worry, I didn't have a hand in leveling any village or massacring civilians. I really just took care of the wounded, both ours and theirs. I never even fired my rifle—the same as Phillip claimed about himself, although he was obviously lying about his experiences. The post-traumatic shock syndrome he's going through now is far worse than anything I suffered. I guess he's not getting the same quality of help I did. I was lucky to have the very best therapist available." Carol had nursed more than his physical wounds; she had helped heal his soul as well.

Deeply disturbed by what he had revealed to her, Beth's voice shook. "Phil hasn't been getting any help—none that I'm aware of. Are you trying to tell me that he has this syndrome, that he's been sick all these years and should have been taking treatment? Damnit, answer me, Joshua," she demanded, pushing out of his arms.

It no longer seemed right to be in Joshua's embrace. She had accepted his caresses and responded to his kisses because of her shock and anger at what Phil had done. Now, she had a horrible suspicion that *she* was culpable, that she had triggered Phil's incredible behavior.

"He's needed expert psychological help, Beth. Maybe he didn't tell you, but I can't believe that he hasn't been seeing a therapist. Beth, if you were thinking of getting married to the man, you must have known him pretty well. How could you be unaware of the symptoms?" He looked incredulous.

"Married? Joshua . . . we really weren't that close. I only went out with him a few times. Even so, you're right. How could I have misinterpreted the signs? Now it's so obvious why he needed me so desperately, why he was so jealous of my attention. Joshua, all of this is my fault . . . ." She gestured impotently at the jumble of equipment strewn around the campsite—at the flares that were guttering to a feeble end.

"Now don't go blaming yourself for what the war did to him, Beth. This has been simmering inside him all along; that's the way it happens with the illness. There was a time bomb in his brain that I bet could have gone off any day."

"But I made it go off *today*. Don't you understand? Phillip loved me and I betrayed him. I turned to you for what I should have found with him. No! Don't touch me," she protested when Joshua tried to put comforting arms around her. "He was ill and I failed him. Joshua, I have to go to Phil and make it up to him. He has to forgive me and let me help him get well again."

Moved by Beth's agony, Joshua put out his hand to touch the honeyed softness of her curls. The condemning glare from her amber eyes stayed him. Despair and hurt roughened his voice. "So you do love him after all, don't you, little girl?" he whispered.

However, the anguished woman didn't hear him. She didn't even feel the spatter of large raindrops that began to raise crown-shaped eruptions of ash in the dust around them. Beth was insensitive to the deluge threatening to fall on her head, but Joshua reacted quickly to the increasing wind. Moving away from her, he hurriedly erected a small tent in the lee of a three-sided rocky outcrop.

After finding the radio Roger had left them, he pulled Beth into the cramped quarters, shutting out the gale-driven rain and the cold of the gloom-filled atmosphere. He insisted that she take off her wet slicker, folding it along with his into one corner.

With a deep sigh, Joshua adjusted his body, seeking a comfortable position for the hour's wait he estimated they had until the helicopter returned.

Beth tried to keep any part of her body from touching

Joshua. But his long legs, drawn up Indian fashion, pressed against her thigh. Even when she shifted against the fabric-covered rock at her end of the tent, there was no room for Beth to move her shoulder away from the hard column of his arm.

In spite of herself, the sheer massive strength of his body made her feel protected and safe. The damp heat that radiated from his skin warmed her guilt-chilled bones and eased tension away from her overstrained muscles.

Feeling the drowsy tendrils of sleep wind around her, Beth tried to fight off the seductive pull of Morpheus's forgetfulness. She had to think, to plan what to do about Phil when she got off the mountain.

She didn't love him—she couldn't marry him—but that didn't absolve her. She had failed him. Somehow, she would have to help him get over the terrible sickness that was clouding his life.

The force of Beth's guilt let her forgive Phil's dangerous disavowal of her and comprehend his violent reaction to stress. She was no longer frightened by his actions now that she understood their roots.

Beth didn't quite know how she would handle the situation, but she was sure that the Veterans Administration would provide Phillip with the medical care he needed.

She wondered if the helicopter had landed in Vancouver yet, and worried about how Phil was dealing with the guilt he must be feeling. He had to be wretchedly depressed.

A small, sighing sound made Beth turn toward Joshua. What she saw infuriated her. Joshua Hunter evidently had no guilty worries plaguing *his* brain. His breathing had slowed to the even cadence of slumber while Beth had sat wrestling with her thoughts.

The ease with which he had fallen asleep made her want to shake him awake. She refused to remember the traumatic night he had spent watching over his father. Nor would she admit that he had worked like a stevedore, loading the helicopter.

Even in the midst of her determinedly righteous indignation, Beth noticed how the dim light had softened the harsh cut of his facial bones. This illusionary roundness of cheek and jaw, combined with his dark, wind-tousled hair, gave her a good idea of what Joshua had looked like when he was ten years old.

Beth squeezed her eyes shut, trying to deny the impact of the emotions this evocative picture generated. But two large tears escaped her desperate attempt at control. They were an homage to his sad childhood and to the loss of something Beth could only dimly acknowledge. The boy she would never see. The son Joshua might have in the future. The sweet child that would never be hers. Bowing her head under the weight of this hurt, Beth slipped into a troubled doze.

When she became aware of her surroundings again, the light in the tent still bordered on stygian darkness and the wind-driven rain continued seeking an opening into the waterproof tenting material.

However, instead of hugging the cold comfort of a rocky niche, Beth found that she was stretched across Joshua's lap, her head pillowed by his shoulder, her body toasting in the heat of his encircling arms. It was obvious that in her exhaustion, she hadn't felt the strong hands that had pulled her off the ground onto sinewy thighs.

With a haziness that mimicked a drug-induced stupor, Beth struggled to focus her eyes and break out of the cocooning safety of Joshua's embrace. The silken bindings that entrapped her instantly metamorphosed into steel cables, as Joshua restrained her efforts.

Not waiting for her to regain complete control of her faculties, Joshua took advantage of her bemused state to kiss her senseless. He didn't allow her to even take a

Hey, great going, Hunter. This charter member welcomes you to the Foot-in-the-Mouth Club, Beth thought, biting her lip to keep from laughing out loud, while watching the tall geologist metaphorically struggle to extract his own king-size appendage.

"Beth . . . Beth, I was only talking about names, for heaven's sake! Theirs are rather high-flown, don't you think?" Relieved that he had regained control of his tongue, Joshua grinned. "And just what makes you so sure that I'd prefer your sisters? What do you know of *my* tastes?"

He looked across the small space that separated them, making an intimate study of her face. A suntanned hand gently touched her hair for a long second, until Beth had the strength to lean away. She felt strangely breathless. How had this innocuous conversation gotten them back to that intense physical awareness they felt for each other?

Frightened, Beth desperately tried to bring reality into focus. "Oh, I know that I'm not your type. I have it on the best authority, Joshua. Yours." He must remember what he had told her last evening.

"You're never going to let me live that down, are you, sweetheart?" A long index finger drew a soft line over her eyebrow. It traced down to her jaw and traversed Beth's lower lip in a sensuous journey that caused her an erotic shiver of anticipation.

Beth grabbed his hand. "Don't do that," she wailed, and then unconsciously placed his work-scarred fingers against her cheek. When she realized what she was doing, she tried to push him away. However, Joshua grabbed her wrist firmly with his other hand. He then compelled her to move his calloused fingertips against the soft bloom of her skin.

"Why are you always making me do things I don't want to?" she entreated him.

Cara's part of the jet set . . . Do they still use that term?'' she asked Joshua, who just shrugged his own ignorance.

"Well, in any case, she's married to a minor count from somewhere or other—Transylvania, I think." With a dramatic swirl, Beth converted her jacket into a cape and draped it in front of her face.

Joshua choked on the coffee he had been in the midst of swallowing. Beth quickly rushed over to pound his back, until he signaled that the coughing fit was under control.

Then struggling to suppress her silly mood, Beth settled into a cross-legged position on the ground and finished her description of her family. "That's a short history of the Cristie girls. Well, hardly short! They're all over five foot nine . . . even my mother. I guess I'm an atavistic throwback to some undernourished ancestor. Or maybe Mom just ran out of steam after having four children in five years. In fact, I'm so different from the others, that if Daddy wasn't such a handsome hunk, I'd be tempted to ask Mom about the postman.''

Beth watched the laughter dance in Joshua's eyes, then her heart lurched when he smiled in appreciation of her exaggerations. She tried not to gasp out loud at the reappearance of the deep dimple in his cheek. It seemed to have the power to make her blood run like lava through her body.

"Hmm. The Three Beauties—Magda, Bianca, Cara," he mused. "And just plain Beth.''

"Just plain Beth?" she echoed in sudden disbelief at the cruel gibe.

Hearing his words repeated, Joshua's face paled. His jaw muscles worked frantically before he rushed on, trying to make up for his verbal clumsiness.

"Well, Beth, I'll bet you beat the pants off those dainty ladies in science and math, and . . . er . . . sports . . .'' He ran down to a miserable stop.

"Glad to see you carry the essentials." Joshua gave a short laugh, but accepted the offering.

He found another rock, three feet away, and began to eat in silence.

Beth was starved, but she tried to control her hunger and appear ladylike. It took her nearly ten minutes to eat half a sandwich.

Joshua watched with growing amazement at her slow progress. He suddenly remembered a story his mother had read to him as a young child, about Mrs. Piggle-Wiggle and the boy who took so long to eat his food that he never finished one meal before it was time for the next.

He couldn't help the chuckle that rose in his throat. When his eyes caught Beth's, she responded with a smothered snicker. Taking another tiny bite, she chewed it until they both burst out laughing.

Beth was elated that her inspired silliness had broken the tension sizzling between them. "It's all my mother's fault. She drove me crazy trying to make a lady of me, like my sisters," she said, feeling that she had to reveal to Joshua a little about her own painful childhood.

"The three of them are her pride and joy—fine arts majors, all. Mom always said that I was a changeling and that she would have given up on having kids if I had come before any of them, instead of last."

Joshua's eyebrow raised, reading a great deal into the bare-bones outline Beth sketched. "Exactly what are these paragons of femininity like?" he asked carefully.

"Oh, truly beautiful—statuesque, with classic features, blue eyes, and ash-blond hair. Probably just your type." Before going on, she gave him a sidelong glance, but just missed the fleeting wash of pain that crossed his face again as he quickly shuttered the emotion away.

"Anyway, the older two, Magda and Bianca, are married to very successful men and have beautiful, perfectly behaved children. The third is a high-fashion model.

"Let's get back to the lahar site. I want to monitor the readings before Roger arrives."

Stumbling away from the rage and pain that radiated from Joshua's face, Beth tried to deny the perverse stab of elation that had zipped through her body when he said that he wasn't married. Yet, why had revealing his marital status made him so angry at her?

She was completely confused. Unless Joshua felt insulted that she could even think he was married. After all, he had kissed her, aroused her, come very close to making love to her. Her suggestion that he was married implied that she thought he really *didn't* have any morals.

Afraid to say anything more that might inflame the situation, Beth hung back while Joshua stalked ahead of her on the trail to the mudflow. She didn't even try to keep up with his long strides.

He still looked furious when she finally reached the site and found him making a quick check of the laser emitter. After watching him for a minute, Beth began to gather her own materials, intending to go back to her base camp for a late lunch.

"Goodbye, Joshua. Hope you find out what's wrong with your equipment," she said softly, slinging her case over her shoulder.

"Where are you going?" Without waiting for any explanation, he abandoned his work to dig into his backpack. "Come on, let's eat. I did promise you lunch," he said gruffly, presenting Beth with a cheese sandwich and indicating a convenient rock seat. "Want some coffee?"

Beth hesitated and then slowly nodded. When she sat down on the hard surface, he poured some of the hot brew into the top of his thermos and carefully passed it to her.

Putting the cup down, Beth dug into her own rucksack. "Raisins and chocolate chip cookies?" she asked, holding out her contribution.

breath as he plunged his tongue into the sweet cavern of her mouth and began searching for the moist treasures contained within.

Her angry "No!" was muffled; her desperate, "Please" was swallowed. Only her sigh of complete capitulation escaped to mock her faltering resolve. Beth could only blame her muddled mind for her fingers opening Joshua's shirt and tracing soft caresses across the silken skin of his naked shoulders. She was equally sure that an unconscious impulse must have taken over her will when she avidly abetted him in the unbuttoning of her own shirt and the placement of his hands on her throbbing breasts.

It was provident that the squawking of the radio receiver ended Beth's attempts to release his devilishly complicated belt buckle . . . for how could she ever rationalize away that revealing action?

Instead of castigating herself for what she had been about to do, her mental defenses allowed her to melt against Joshua's bare chest and hold on to him while he searched the space around them for the radio.

Joshua tried to regulate his ragged breathing so that he could answer the call when he finally found the device. His ironic chuckle, and the shaky hand he passed over Beth's hair, documented the struggle he was having in regaining control. Harsh reality finally sobered him when he checked the glowing dials of his watch and found out how much time had passed in exhausted sleep.

"What in the hell's gone wrong?" he muttered when he saw it was almost one o'clock, and that three hours had slipped by.

Leaning over, he unzipped the tent flap, using the extra light to help him adjust the reception frequency. The garbled noise became discernible words. "Mount St. Helens, this is Lone Star-Oil . . . come in please. Over."

Joshua depressed the transmit button. "Lone Star-Oil,

this is Mount St. Helens. We read you. What's going on, Roger? Over.''

''Joshua, we had one hell of a time getting down here. Turbulence was horrendous, and we had to set down three or four times to wait out the worst of the storm. Also, our friend with the gun went bonkers toward the end, completely round the bend. Mr. Hunter managed to conk him unconscious with his boot. Price has been carted off to Portland. A severe anxiety attack, the medics said. Over.''

Joshua didn't protest when Beth lifted herself away from him. Her stiff body eloquently conveyed the shame and agony Roger's revelation had generated within her.

Beth tried to blank out the last few minutes with Joshua from her memory, making believe they had never happened. She retreated to the resolutions she had made before falling asleep. Phil and his actions were totally her responsibility. She would devote herself to seeing him well again. There could be no one else in her life until that happened. She let the radio exchange wash over her.

''Roger, we read you. How is everything else? How is my dad? Over.''

''Your father and Ms. Murray are fine. She insisted that he go to the hospital for a check-up, but he was looking fit. Dana Clark was shaken up a bit, but I'm going to ask her out for a drink tonight, to make up for the bumpy ride. Over.''

''Fine, Roger, fine. Thanks for that important bit of information, but when will you get up here to collect us insignificant folk? What's taking so long? Over.''

''That's the bad news, Josh. No flights into the restricted zone . . . period. You have so much turbulence up there, we can't get clearance. They'll let us pick you up at a point outside it as long as the light holds, but you're going to have to hike ten miles to get there. The good news is that the Geologic Survey is sure no event is in the works—just more ash and tremors . . . no magma and no explosion. Over.''

"So that's the good news, huh? Roger, with all this ash and rain, we can't make ten miles safely before nightfall. We'll have to use the southeast escape route. Remember it? We'll camp about six miles from here. Beth and I can get that far before dark. But we'll have to spend the night. Tomorrow, we'll hike to the alternate pickup point we mapped out. Be there at nine in the morning. And Roger . . . remind them that my equipment predicted that there *will* be a small event, but hopefully not before you get us off, OK? Over.''

"I'll tell them, Josh. See you at nine tomorrow morning. Good luck. Over and out.''

"Over and out.''

Beth had registered the conversation between Joshua and Roger and fully understood its impact. Somehow the trial ahead of her was only fit punishment for the guilt she felt. She almost looked forward to the hardship. It would keep her mind away from the insidious temptation the man held for her. The pain of the hike would focus her attention on her most immediate goal, to get off the mountain and get Phillip well again.

"OK, Beth, we've got to get our feet moving. It's quite a trek, but we're going to use the safest way out. Don't worry, even if the volcano blows ahead of my prediction, we'll be all right,'' he assured her, sounding supremely confident. "Let's get some supplies together.''

She responded immediately to his suggestion, happy to focus her thoughts on survival.

Outside the shelter, the rain had slackened off and the wind had gentled to mild eddies. In the respite, they made backpacks for the trip. Joshua prepared a relatively light burden for Beth, including two wool blankets wrapped around some freeze-dried packets of food.

When he helped Beth shoulder the pack, Joshua finally acknowledged the tears that fell quietly and relentlessly down her cheeks.

"We can't control who we love, or who loves us." His eyes were as enigmatic as his words. "Beth, I . . . Oh hell, Beth . . ."

Some censor in his brain had clamped down and the soft sound of her name was abruptly cut off when he turned away from her.

In a frenzy of motion, Joshua filled two large canteens with water and then stowed equipment into his own backpack, including the tent and the one sleeping bag that hadn't been stowed into the helicopter.

His energetic preparations touched off a strange compulsion in Beth. She also began rummaging through the equipment until she triumphantly held up her catchall cosmetic bag. Somehow, finding it lifted her spirits dramatically, to the point where her tears dried up and she could even banter with Joshua when he questioned her puzzling activity.

"What's that, Beth?"

"Can't go anywhere without my makeup kit. What would Mother say?" She laughed until dark thoughts were pushed aside.

"Come on, you can do without lipstick for one day."

"Absolutely not. Besides, there's lots of other things I need: a nail file, cleansing cream, hairbrush, toothbrush . . . bandages. After all, one never can tell when one is going to fall over a misplaced experiment and get a scrape or two, can one?" she chided.

"OK, OK, don't rub it in," he chuckled. "But you can carry it. That suitcase must weigh a ton."

Wrinkling her upturned nose at him, Beth hooked the small bag onto her belt. With that final task completed, they were ready to leave. The two again put on the hooded slickers they had used during the packing. The waterproof material would keep the worst of the rain and clinging ash off them and their supplies.

Beth handed Joshua a face mask, but instead of tying it on, he grabbed her hand, pulling her toward him. His startled eyes seemed as surprised as her own. Joshua looked as if finding her in his arms was the last thing he had expected—or wanted.

Then Beth's name was uttered in a stifled groan and his mouth captured hers. For a long moment, the drum of her heart was louder than the rain pounding down with re-newed fury. However, its wet force finally brought back harsh reality. With the strength of desperation, Beth wrenched free of Joshua to stumble down the trail.

"Wait, Beth, that's the wrong way," he shouted after her.

"It's away from you—and that's where I've got to go, anywhere you're not," she threw back over her shoulder. "You keep grabbing what doesn't belong to you. To me, you're like the plague—something contagious and deadly," she yelled into the wind, breaking into a reckless run.

Joshua easily caught up to her with those incredibly long strides of his and roughly pulled her around to face his rage. The fierceness of his features matched the fury of the elemental sky and earth. To Beth, he seemed as dangerous as the rain-drenched, percolating volcano that was waiting for her to falter, to make the slightest mistake in judgment.

"All right, you've goddamn well made your point, lady. Don't worry, I'll get you off this mountain so you can get back to that crazy man you love so much. I'll not touch you again—not if you beg me to. Now come on with me, you're turning right into hell this way." He strode off in the opposite direction, not looking back to see if she followed.

But she did trek after him—if not to perdition, then into a future that might not be much different, as she settled into a defeated walk, trailing in Joshua Hunter's giant footsteps.

_____ NINE _____

Harmonic tremors moved through the earth, miles below. Beth couldn't feel those vibrations, but she was very aware of the rolling earth beneath her feet when a minor earthquake rumbled down the trail.

She and Joshua had been walking for almost two and a half hours. The actual path they followed was invisible under an inch of gray, swirling ash. It was treacherous, but until now, caution and instinct had kept them safe. However, in the next step, Beth stumbled on an unseen pebble, and when she tried to right herself, her flailing arms made a desperate grab for the bulge of Joshua's backpack, strapped under his slicker.

"I'm so sorry." She gasped the apology as the unexpected counterforce of her hands caused him to stagger, propelling them both into the sticky, wet grit.

The rain and wind had continued in unpredictable gusts during the hike. It had stopped a few minutes ago, but with the heat of her exertions steaming her clothing under the slicker, Beth had never been so miserably uncomfortable in her life.

She felt tears of exhaustion filling up her eye-saving

goggles. Lifting them away from her cheeks, the moisture coursed downward, leaving a meander of clean streaks that again gave the crazy-clown look to the rest of her dirty face. However, this time, Joshua didn't try to erase the grime. He just looked at the damage done to her features and got up slowly. The nearly six miles they had covered since one-thirty had taken their toll, even on his endurance-trained muscles.

The actual distance, the real difficulty of the hike, had been minimal. What had tired Joshua, and exhausted Beth, had been the tension of not knowing just what was under each footfall in the thick, wet ash. The gray-out, which blended path, rock, mountain, and sky into a traitorous, monotonous monochrome, had added to the pressure.

Beth felt totally disheartened. Even though Joshua had predicted there were at least eighteen hours before any event, she knew they needed to get as far as they could this afternoon, in order to make the last few miles to the pick-up point in the morning. But they were fast running out of daylight and Beth couldn't go a single step farther.

"Joshua, please go on ahead. I'm not going to be able to keep up anymore, and I know you've been slowed down enough by me already," she pleaded.

"No, I'm not going to leave you! I'll get you out safely. If nothing else, I can do that," he vowed. He knew the intensity of his declaration mystified and frightened Beth. Joshua could see it in her eyes. Well, he didn't care how scared she felt right now if it produced enough adrenaline to get her going again. He was not going to let another woman die on this mountain because of him.

"We'll stop about a half mile down from here. Six hundred steps. Come on, lady, get up." He pulled the shaking woman to her feet. "You be point. I'll hang on to your belt. Come on now, lead!" he ordered.

Instead of holding on to her jacket's belt, Beth found that Joshua was actually supporting much of her weight, with his large, capable hands spanning her waist.

The responsibility of finding safe footfalls helped Beth make the next two hundred steps; after that, her mind grew numb and she stopped counting. But just as her second wind completely deserted her, Joshua called a halt.

They were amid huge rocks, in a flat area at the edge of a narrow ravine. He looked around the boulder-strewn clearing in the last sickly-gray light of the shortened spring day. "This is a good place to pitch the tent. At least the rain seems to have stopped for now. The rocks will give us some protection from this wind and reflect back the heat from our fire. Let's find some kindling."

"If nothing else, Mount St. Helens has an unlimited supply of seasoned wood," Beth said lightly. It was an effort for her to attempt this mundane conversation, but in the forced march they had just made, much of Beth's anger and fear had been sublimated into the energy needed to keep up. She didn't want to spend her remaining time with Joshua in fighting.

Looking at the cleft in the ground, Beth had a flash of intuition. "Joshua, that wouldn't be the start of Ape Canyon over there, would it?"

When he nodded, she laughed. "Well, maybe we could hire a couple of those Big Foot dudes to carry us to the pick-up point tomorrow."

Joshua just stared at her, obviously not appreciating her attempt at humor. Beth shrugged when he finally grunted some sort of response and then bent to construct a fire ring. She wasn't sure if he was just tired, or still actively mad at her. Too weary herself to challenge him, she found as much firewood as she could carry and dropped it beside the ring of rocks he was forming.

After it was finished, Joshua went to collect his own

armful of wood, dumping the far larger amount on top of Beth's contribution. Using his boot, he then cleared a space around their impromptu hearth. Together, they raised the tent, working in unconscious harmony. Then Joshua unrolled the sleeping bag and temporarily placed it near the fire he had started.

Realizing how quickly the remaining light was disappearing, Joshua finally broke his silence. "We'd better eat and get settled before nightfall. That could be in just a few minutes with this ash," he muttered. "I put the sleeping bag next to the fire to dry out. We can do that, too, while we're eating."

He stared at the bag for a minute. The material nearest the fire ring toasted in the luxury of the flames, while the far corners absorbed the cold of the Mount St. Helens twilight. It would have to serve as a combination couch and dining table and—later—as a bed. But his mind shied away from that disturbing thought.

Joshua's temper seemed to have improved—barely, Beth thought. But she acknowledged his advice with a nod and then pulled off the sticky slicker that had protected her clothing. Before she got the food out of her backpack, Beth poured a spare amount of water from her canteen and wiped off the grime from her face and hands.

She rummaged in the maligned cosmetic bag for her hairbrush, using it to vigorously cleanse the ash from her short curls. Finding her toothbrush, she put a drop of water and a thin strip of toothpaste on it, brushing, and then stoically swallowing the remains.

"I wonder how much nutritive value fluoride provides, Joshua," she jested, once again trying to ease the tension between them.

This time, Joshua responded with a humorous contribution of his own. "I don't know about that, but you'll probably never have to worry about ulcers now. Can I have a shot?"

Beth laughed and then put a dab of toothpaste on his outstretched finger. He scrubbed away, swallowing with a grimace. Knowing that it would make him feel better, she offered him her hairbrush, which he used to rid his scalp of the itchy particles.

Rubbing his day's accumulation of beard, he ventured speculatively, "You wouldn't happen to have a razor in that magic bag, would you?"

With a theatrical gesture, Beth dumped the whole contents out on the bed roll. Joshua made a tally of useful items as she slowly put everything back.

"No, no razor, but . . ." She gleefully produced a small tube of chemical depilatory.

Joshua chuckled deep in his chest. She was a delight, he thought. "You'll do, Beth, you'll do. However, I think I'll pass and stick with the whiskers."

Trying not to let him see just how happy his praise had made her, Beth broke out the rations for the evening meal. "We have corned beef, peaches, instant coffee, and some cookies," she informed him.

After dividing the food portions, Beth pulled out collapsible metal cups and shook packets of coffee crystals into them, swirling water around to help the particles dissolve. While the brew heated on the top log, they ate in silence. This time the quiet was not filled with anger, just exhaustion.

When they were done, Beth neatly put away the used foil packaging. "I'd feel guilty leaving this trash. I guess the anti-litter people have done well with their advertising campaigns."

"Oh, I'm sure even they would understand, under these circumstances." Joshua leaned back against the boulder behind him, his long legs folded, hands on his knees. He looked out at the dead gray world. This must have been a glorious view of Mount St. Helens in her better days, but now the darkening sky and ash-covered rocks offered no point of focus. "It's going to be a long night," he grunted.

"We could tell each other our life's story," Beth suggested. "Mine should take at least five minutes." She looked speculatively at Joshua's face. "Yours would probably last us until morning, I'd guess."

A startling mixture of longing and pain crossed his face, and Beth knew she had just said the wrong thing. Damn! she swore to herself, would she never learn?

But his response surprised her. "I have a variation. Pick a year, any year, and then try to remember everything you can from it in detail. The younger you were, the more points you get."

"Hey, I used to do that when I was too tired to read but couldn't sleep. I'm pretty good at it," she boasted.

"We'll see," he warned. "You go first, if you're so good."

"OK. I think I'll try for quality, not quantity. The very earliest thing I remember is when I was less than two. Let's see . . . I'm in a small apartment, and my crib is against the wall, to the right of the entry door. There's a big window to the left. An alcove across from me is the kitchenette. I'm fascinated by what appear to be stars on the darkened ceiling of that area. My parents' and sisters' rooms must be to my right. No one is there. I feel all alone and I start to cry." Beth checked Joshua's face for his reaction.

"Not bad, not too bad, if true," he challenged.

"Oh, it's true, all right. I described the place to my mother and she couldn't believe it. She said that I was twenty months old when we moved from the apartment to our first house. How about twenty-five points for that one?"

"That's fair enough." He smiled. "OK, my turn. I think I'll try for a big score, too. My third year was very traumatic. It started with my mother threatening me with having to wash my own diapers if I didn't shape up and get myself potty trained.''

Beth's hoot of laughter bounced around the rocks. It died a sudden death when she gave Joshua's arm a mock punch, and he abruptly pulled back from the contact. Remembering that she had set up the parameters, Beth bit off any reference to his hurtful response.

"Go on," she murmured instead.

He shifted again on the sleeping bag, and it seemed to Beth that he was putting even more distance between them.

"My brother, Carter, made his appearance that year in February. I recall sitting at the top of the stairs at my aunt Lil's house, eating a bowl of cereal and crying. I knew that my parents had gone off somewhere, to get a sister or brother for me, but I really wasn't too thrilled about having any competition." He chuckled. "Carter turned out to be all right, though. He slept all the time and didn't bug me until I was ten or so. He literally dozed through the first decade and a half of his life. We didn't know he was saving his strength for his fifteenth birthday, when he discovered girls. I don't think he's gotten any sleep since."

Beth interrupted. "You've mentioned your brother a couple of times. Where is he now?"

"He's in Saudi Arabia this month. He's an engineer and travels around the world for Dad, trouble-shooting the foreign-based projects. Carter pops back for a few days between assignments. He's still a bachelor and seems to love the footloose life." Joshua shook his head as if it were the last thing *he* would like.

In fact, his reaction implied that home, hearth, and wife were all he craved. That last sentence echoed in Beth's ears: his *brother* was still a bachelor. It was as if Joshua had placed himself into another category entirely.

Of course, Joshua's exact marital status had to be the

cause of his mysterious behavior—his declaration that he was not free. Had a marriage recently been dissolved against his wishes? Or was he involved in a hopeless affair?

Finding out his secret had become an almost overwhelming compulsion, though Beth knew that she had no business prying. She didn't even have the right to listen to Joshua if he decided to tell her what was causing him so much pain. There was another man she had to worry about and there was no place in her life for anyone else right now.

"Let's see, back to year three," Joshua was saying. "In March, we got Charlie, the Airedale. Now that was the best dog a kid could ever wish for. Why, he was so smart, he even taught me to read," he informed Beth with a straight face."

"Oh, come on, Joshua. This is supposed to be fact, not fiction."

"No, really, Beth. I would lay on the rug with a comic book or *Winnie the Pooh,* and Charlie would point out a word with his nose and tell me what it was."

"That's impossible," Beth denied emphatically.

"Let me give you some examples: 'Ruff,' he'd say, about Eyoore's troubles; 'Roof,' he told me, when I wanted to know where Piglet was during the big rainstorm.

" 'Harff,' he answered, after I asked how much Pooh should eat, when he was also trapped by the storm with a dwindling supply of honey."

Beth laid her head back against the rock and groaned with laughter. "Twenty-five big ones for year three, Joshua. That's even better than your father's *Mar-doc.*"

She smiled up at his face, which was glowing in the firelight. *Lord, he's so attractive,* she thought. To her, he was the most beautiful man in the world.

Recalling her first reaction to him on the day they met, Beth felt it wash over her again. She was ashamed that she couldn't seem to control her longing for him. So desirable, and yet he was so utterly unobtainable that he might as well be an erotic fantasy from her overactive libido.

A heavy pulse under his jaw caught her attention, and Beth's eyes followed that strong line of bone back to his dark hair. It had gone three weeks past a definite need for cutting, curling over his ear. The wayward strands evoked an image of the three-year-old Joshua teaching himself to read, with the help of his dog, of course.

Not really thinking, just feeling, Beth leaned forward and kissed the lobe, just where his hair ended. Instantly aghast at what she had done, she sat back on her heels and fearfully watched his face for a reaction.

When he finally responded, his voice contained no anger, just weariness. "You don't play fair, Beth. You change the rules as you go along."

With ears burning from chagrin, Beth tried to make light of her aggression. "No, Joshua, that was just in honor of your third year. Congratulations, I award you the contest."

"No, it's your turn again. We need another round to certify the champion," he insisted coolly. But Joshua knew that the only thing cool about him at the moment was his voice. All it had taken was the brush of her lips on his ear to set his blood boiling. While he understood that she hadn't really meant the gesture to be seductive, he was very close to losing the thin thread of control that was barely keeping him from pulling her under him. "Go on with your next entry, Beth," he urged in desperation.

Hearing the tension in Joshua's voice, Beth moved away from him, placing needed inches between her body, hot with embarrassment, and his cold one. She sat against the rapidly chilling boulder, using the temperature gradient to transfer heat away from herself.

"Oh, all right." She reluctantly gave in to his insistence

and hurriedly recalled another year. "When I was nine, I fell in love with dinosaurs."

She fell silent for a second, abruptly realizing just what she had revealed: perhaps the most cherished memory of her youth. She had never told anyone about that fascination—it had meant too much to her. The compulsion had filled lonely childhood hours, letting her forget the rejection of parents and escape the taunting rivalry of three beautiful sisters.

Looking into the puzzled eyes of the man next to her, Beth took a shuddering breath. She *wanted* him to know, to give to him a small, but immensely important, part of herself. Because there was nothing else of any value he could ever have from her.

The gift from her soul spilled out in a gush of revelation. "That year, I read everything I could find about dinosaurs—all the books in the school library, and everything I could buy. I spent long, happy hours fantasizing about the expeditions I would lead, and marvelous days devising ways of taming them. I wasn't just fascinated with the magnificent beasts, I truly loved them. They were my secret passion. Nobody knew how important they were to me, so nobody could try to steal them away."

The ache in Beth's voice told Joshua more than he could bear to know about her childhood. He remembered what Ruth had said about Beth's family, and he could imagine how three daunting older sisters and a pair of insensitive parents could have stolen away many of her dreams. He found himself wanting to take her into his arms, and tell her that he would fulfill every wish she had ever had. However, he could do nothing but sit there, listening to the rest of Beth's remembrance.

"For some strange reason," she was saying, "it took me a long time to discover that they were already gone . . . extinct. When it finally sank into my head that I had missed them by sixty million years, I was inconsolable. I mourned their demise for months. Nobody could figure out what was wrong with me.

"Luckily, just before I perished from a broken heart . . ." Beth grinned sardonically at Joshua's raised eyebrow, "I discovered *Lost Continent* by Arthur Conan Doyle, and then H. G. Wells's *War of the Worlds*. My life was saved by science fiction. Not only were there lots of dinosaurs running around on its pages, there were also all kinds of lovely Bug-eyed Monsters. Of course, that was before the genre was respectable for little girls to read, and everybody was really sure that I'd gone round the bend."

Joshua's delighted laughter thrilled Beth. The attractive sound eased the tension that had been growing in the small arc of light thrown out by the twisting flames. The honest admiration Beth saw in his eyes when he finally stopped chuckling helped her recover a lot of the self-worth she had lost in the last few days.

Smiling with the infamous grin that Phil had wanted to keep for his exclusive enjoyment, Beth finished her contest story. "I guess my love of dinosaurs led me to study paleontology, and then ecology. And, of course, I've developed an incurable addiction for science fiction."

"You're quite a woman, Beth." Joshua voiced what had been in his eyes. There might be more there, but complete darkness had fallen and it was hard for Beth to interpret their flickering depth in the unreliable firelight.

"You know, I shudder to think what would happen if we really met up with one of your Bug-eyed Monsters out there in space someday. How will we ever communicate with something truly different when our own species has so much trouble understanding one another."

"But, Joshua, wouldn't it be wonderful to find them anyway? Sometimes I could just cry when I think about the things I'll never know about our universe—all the wonders that are waiting for us if we manage to survive the next few decades.''

Beth was fleetingly aware that she and Joshua had finally been able to converse on a level that had nothing to do with the intense attraction they felt for each other.

"Terra incognita," he murmured.

"Exactly," Beth said, smiling at his reference to what the Spanish explorers had written on their maps to signify unknown lands. "That mysterious territory has always thrilled my imagination, while scaring the spit out of my mouth. That's what saddens me, Joshua." She sighed. "The fact that I'll never get to travel that marvelous deep, with all its angels and devils."

"Or with a friendly, intelligent dinosaur or two?" he chuckled.

"That, too," she admitted. Beth contemplated the images dancing in the fire for a long moment, almost seeing the shape of a mythical salamander grinning at her from the flames.

As the wind increased its intensity, a high, keening sound seemed to bound from boulder to boulder. Big Foot coming to toss a few rocks on them? Beth found that she was too tired to worry very much about the thought.

Yawning widely she said, "Your turn again, Joshua." Exhaustion was creeping up on her, but the contest was unresolved.

"No, I concede the match to the dinosaurs and our space friends. God, I'm tired. Let me bank the fire and get this sleeping bag spread out in the tent."

After Joshua dealt with the fire, Beth helped him open up the down-filled bag. When it was properly smoothed out, he handed her one of the wool blankets they had brought with them.

"Good night," he said as they settled into the small enclosure. Without another word, he wrapped himself in his own cover and turned on his side, facing away from Beth.

She looked at him lying there, his long legs sticking out of the too-short material. Suppressing a deep sigh, Beth rolled up in her own blanket. Resting with her head cradled on her arms, she realized that Joshua had placed an imaginary, upright sword in the small space that separated their bodies.

She was thankful for his tact. Yet somehow, the thought of his strong arms keeping her fears at bay was enormously appealing. Tears might have remedied the situation: big crocodile drops, along with wracking sobs. No man could resist comforting a crying woman. However, she did have her pride!

At any rate, she was also very tired. Exhaustion proved the perfect sleeping pill and an anodyne to her terror. Closing her eyes, she fell asleep almost immediately.

Strange dreams kept pulling Beth to the edge of awareness. Dreams again featuring a beautiful blond girl dressed in white and surrounded by a bright-blue light. The young woman beckoned to Beth, her lips moving as she desperately tried to communicate something very important to her.

But Beth forgot all about the dreams—all about the girl—when deep in the night, she awoke to the sickening, rocking motion of an earthquake. It was larger in magnitude than anything she had experienced on the mountain, but maybe that was because they were closer to the point of origin. Beth didn't know.

"Joshua, is this it?" she called out, somehow sure that he was awake. "Is an eruption going to happen now?" Beth turned to face him, trying to keep the fear out of her voice.

"I'm not sure; this just started. I think it's only another tremor. Don't worry, my instruments were right. We should be OK until tomorrow morning. Anyway, we can't go out there now. Listen to that rain—we couldn't see a thing.''

Even as he spoke, the ground settled. Beth found herself waiting long, tense seconds for any hint of renewed activity.

"What time is it?" she finally asked. Then, not waiting for Joshua's answer, she reached out for the watch strapped to his wrist. Finding it by some sort of instinct, Beth read the glowing dial. "One-thirty. How long have you been up?"

"I don't think I've been asleep; overtired," he confessed.

"Overtired and freezing, Joshua. Your hand is like ice. That blanket is way too short for you; let's share mine," she offered.

"No . . . it's all right. The cold doesn't bother me. I'm used to a lot worse. You're the one who's shaking. Beth, don't be afraid, I'll get you out, I promise," he soothed. "Just go back to sleep, I'll be OK," he insisted.

"Nonsense! You have to lead us down tomorrow, and I don't want to rely on a blurry-eyed icicle."

"OK, I guess you're right. Come over here."

When Beth moved next to him, Joshua used his own blanket to cover his long legs and then spread Beth's over both their bodies.

Trying to live up to her own rules, Beth fought the temptation to snuggle into Joshua's arms. Instead, she just curled up against his side with her back to him. Within a few seconds, his nearness had calmed her racing heart and reassured her frightened mind.

In return, Beth felt warmth transfer from her body to the cold material of his clothing. In less than five minutes, Joshua's steady, even breathing told her that she had done the right thing; the chill had been keeping a very tired man awake.

Smiling, she fell back to sleep soon afterward.

TEN

The ghostly-gray light confused Beth when she opened her eyes. After her vision finally cleared, she found that her brain was waging a war with her body.

Sometime during the night, Joshua must have turned toward her. He now lay in an exhaustion-begotten oblivion, with his head on her shoulder, his right arm around her waist, and the fingers of his left hand just touching her cheek.

That provoking arm in front of her eyes became the unwanted focus of Beth's detailed examination of a rough wool sleeve and a large, suntanned hand. Why the combination was so interesting and appealing to her defied conscious analysis.

The phosphorescent hands of Joshua's watch told her that it was five-thirty. Her head was screaming at her that they should be getting up to leave before the volcano did whatever it was that it was going to do, according to Joshua's theory. By contrast, Beth's body told her to melt, to stroke his prominent wrist bones and to kiss the union joining his long thumb to the rest of his hand.

The intense internal conflict finally made her laugh out

loud. Being turned on by an opposable thumb was just too ridiculous in their precarious situation.

At the sound of her amusement, Joshua turned in his deep sleep. That positioned his lean body so it mostly covered Beth's. His mouth pressed against her throat, and with his long legs entangling her shorter ones, his hard body became a disturbingly welcome weight on hers.

Nuzzling her neck, he murmured softly. The words were indecipherable, but the content became obvious when his mouth moved sensuously along her skin, sending waves of shivers down her spine.

Knowing that she should gracefully cough or slip out of his arms didn't help Beth. The barrier he had erected between them last night should have made her separate their bodies with a cooling distance, yet she just didn't have the ability to move away.

Beth had never felt like this before. This man's touch actually thrilled her. She loved the feel of his heavy thighs on hers. They were exciting, even through the two layers of rough fabric that separated their skin.

Realizing that she would never get another chance to be so close to him, Beth's eyes devoured the planes and angles of Joshua's handsome face. Unable to control herself, her fingers traced the curve of his dark eyebrow and the harsh strength of his jaw. She touched his forehead lightly, pushing the shaggy dark hair away from his closed eyes—eyes that abruptly opened and focused on her face.

Joshua groaned, but he couldn't help gripping Beth's shoulders and moving more fully on top of her. He knew who this was; there was no confusion in his mind with the woman in the nightmare he had just had. Even though Carol had called to him this very night—her mouth silently working, a blue aura of sorrow encircling her—he knew who he wanted to hold now.

Although Joshua was aware that he had no right to be doing this, he didn't stop. He could feel the heat of his body burn through the flannel and denim of Beth's clothes and meet her own warmth. Fire concentrated in the area where his male presence began to pulse and grow. She couldn't help but be aware of the full extent of his need, but she made no move to pull away and Joshua could no longer do it on his own.

Beth felt Joshua's hot mouth trail her neck, capturing her lips in a searching, devouring kiss that she was unable to resist. Her automatic impulse to fight him off died in the intensity with which he consumed her mouth and probed its interior. The adamant avowal she had made yesterday, telling him that he didn't have the right to touch her, to arouse her, now seemed to have been spoken by someone else.

The woman she had been the day before had never experienced the overwhelming need to writhe against the weight of a fully aroused male body, striving for throbbing contact with the core of her feminine existence.

Beth had turned into such an uncontrolled being. When the length of Joshua's tongue stroked hers, the moist heat of it threatened to ignite her, to rocket her body straight through to the erotic explosion she had never felt before.

The sound of her muffled groan made Joshua think that she was protesting his embrace. He abruptly pulled his mouth off hers and searched the glowing gold of her eyes. But what he read on her face darkened his own multicolored irises.

Burying his long fingers in the short tousle of her hair, Joshua tried to dampen the passion that was shaking both of them. "Beth, oh, my darling . . . you've got to stop me. This shouldn't be happening!" he pleaded.

However, before she could form a word of disagreement, he was bruising her lips with the force of his mouth, pushing the delicate tissues against her teeth. It was as if he were trying to frighten her with the power he barely controlled.

But when Beth refused to be cowed by his attack and returned the pressure—strength for strength—Joshua shuddered his capitulation. He turned his kiss into a soft, sweet seduction of moist mouth and honey-coated tongue.

In utter abandon to the compelling sweep of the desire she felt, Beth clasped Joshua against herself, holding his broad back fiercely, her arms straining to pull him closer.

She wanted him desperately, and nothing else—nobody else—mattered at that moment. Beth had never felt anything so strongly in her life. The men in her past had been dim images of what she had been unconsciously searching for. Joshua was the epitome of that quest.

He also seemed consumed in a tortured desire. Whatever curse had been holding him in its frightful thrall had become powerless against the tide of passion that was shaking his body. His hands frantically touched Beth and his mouth dropped burning kisses through the barrier of her clothes.

Caught up in the necessity to caress him, Beth unbuttoned his shirt, slipping searching fingers inside to the soft down of dark hair. His chest was that surprising male construct of hard and smooth. The unyielding, flat muscles of uncompromising strength were covered by skin of a masculine satin that was warm and electric to her wandering hands.

"Oh, my God, Beth!" he groaned to her. "I can't bear this. I won't have the strength to stop in another second."

Complying when his eyes demanded a response, she replied, "I don't want you to stop." Pulling at his shirt, she tugged it out of the confining waistband of his jeans.

At the touch of her slim fingers moving over his flat stomach, Joshua began to tremble. In a moaning frenzy, he undid her shirt, exposing small, firm breasts to his hungry gaze. Her nipples hardened when he touched her skin lightly with his lips and then tantalized it with the tender caresses of his fingers, all along her shivering front.

"Are you cold, sweetheart?" His voice was rough and hoarse. She shook her head no, and then nodded yes: both hot and cold, by turns.

"Then let me warm you in the best way possible." Rolling away from her for an instant, Joshua raised up on his knees and slipped out of his shirt. Then he awkwardly tugged off his denim jeans.

Beth filled her starving eyes with his magnificent form as he slowly revealed its secrets. Her gaze followed the hair on his chest where it veed down to the brief, sexy shorts he wore. Lean, long legs were adorned by the same dark covering, but there was nothing of animal hairiness to his body. Rather, it was the finishing touch to his perfection.

However, when he turned slightly, Beth found that his beauty had been marred. Snaring her attention like a fiery brand was a long scar that ran from just under his right arm to the midline of his body.

Noticing the questioning care in her eyes, Joshua laughed with a negligence only time could give to near disaster. "I didn't manage to duck every time, sweetheart."

The thought that something might have kept her from ever meeting Joshua generated a moist glow in the large eyes that pulled at him with the force of an undeniable want. Seeing the fear and desire mirrored in those amber jewels, he uttered the strangled cry of a man truly lost. Quickly kneeling before her, Joshua frantically helped Beth out of the clothing that kept her exquisite proportions from his eyes.

"You . . . are . . . so . . . beautiful!" he enunciated, as if his mouth was reluctant to part with the savoring sentence. "Your skin is so soft, like warm velvet." His long, gentle fingers stroked her arms and shoulders.

"Your breasts are perfect," he avowed.

Blushing at his praise, Beth couldn't help noticing that his large hands had no trouble covering them. His fingers moved on, encircling the small measure of her waist, touching the taut flatness of her stomach and the smooth roundness of her hips.

"You have marvelous pelvic bones," his whisper teased in a clinical tone designed to ease her embarrassment. "And while you're such a little thing, your marvelous legs seem to go on forever," he said, stroking all along their length.

Joshua delicately surveyed her thighs, stopping to linger here and touch there until Beth grabbed his hands and pulled him back to lie at her side. It was her turn to drive Joshua crazy with her mouth and fingers.

Kissing his lovely, prominent collarbones, she nuzzled his neck and then arched like a cat against the sudden pulsing she felt where their bodies pressed together.

Halting her sensuous rubbing, Joshua reached down to pull off his shorts, throwing them to a corner of the tent.

When he took her into his arms again, Beth's fingers began a serpentine journey down Joshua's body. It ended abruptly when she encountered the thick and hard measure of the man. Instead of intimately stroking him as she wanted to do, a sudden terror made her fingers tremble so badly that she struggled away from his arms with desperate strength.

Seeing the unquestionable fear on her face grooved a line between Joshua's eyebrows.

Beth turned away from his gaze, her breath coming in short little pants. Instead of the recriminations she expected, gentle hands began to massage the tense muscles of her shoulders; Joshua's coaxing was a warm whisper in her ear.

"I need you so much, my darling. It's been so long, Beth. Please don't deny me. This is something that only you can give."

Nothing had prepared her for his words. She wasn't sure if he meant them in the physical or emotional sense, but the quiet force of his statement shimmered in her brain. She finally acknowledged what she had intuitively known since the day she first set eyes on him. *He* was the man she had been waiting for all these years.

With that realization, Beth knew that there was no way she could deny him her body's expression of her feelings. But what made her hesitate now was the sure knowledge that the passion they would experience together would be binding for her. By making love with Joshua, she would be pledging herself to him completely, for the rest of her life.

And all he had spoken of was need.

Faced with making a total commitment to him, Beth found that she wanted to share all the old vows that went with the pledging of love: for richer, for poorer; for better or worse; in sickness and in health.

But Joshua had not spoken of love or lasting commitment. Did she dare chance this ultimate bonding to him and then have him leave her? Could she survive knowing that she would never have his embrace again, never to be able to find another love like this for the rest of her life?

She tried to explain her misgivings to Joshua. "Oh, my dearest, I want to come to you," she shuddered. "But I'm afraid of what will happen to me . . . of what you will do to me . . ."

Her voice faltered, fearing that she wasn't explaining it to him very well. Her fears seemed too nebulous and confusing to be put into a logical statement that Joshua could understand. His next words confirmed her inability to express herself.

"You don't mean that Price hurt you . . . that you're afraid of making love with me?" Joshua, struggling to decipher her meaning, had gone off on an unrelated tangent.

"Phil? No, we never even . . . I've never wanted to . . . with anyone before."

"Lord! So *that's* what Price meant. No wonder he tried to shoot me, the poor bastard." He sympathized and exalted at the same time. "Ah, darling, don't be afraid. I'll keep you safe," he crooned soothingly into her ear. "It'll be good; it'll be wonderful. Just trust me. Say that you trust me," he implored.

Puzzling as it was, Beth could see that Joshua's emotional need for her to trust in him was almost as strong as his physical desire. When she gave her affirmation with a nod of her head, he crushed her to him, his eyes squeezed shut with relief.

Laying her back down on the sleeping bag, Joshua tried to control his shaking body so that he could fulfill his promise to Beth not to hurt her.

He had never made love to a virgin before. Hell, after a dozen years, he wasn't much better than a novice himself. Nevertheless, he would do everything in his power to hold back, to bring Beth to the glory she had saved for him.

He began to slowly stroke her, to lead her through a complete course in loving passion, while trying to remember all the secrets he once had known.

Touching Beth's hair with tender fingers, he praised her while he kissed the curls near her ear. "Your hair is so soft. I love rubbing my cheek against it. And oh, how wonderful your skin is. Don't you feel the contrast of my rough on your smooth? Doesn't that thrill you, darling?"

Beth nodded her agreement against the silken hair of his chest. In fact, her nerves had become so incredibly sensitized that her world became a sensual arena of opposites.

Her fingertips compared the hard muscles of Joshua's back to the soft springiness of his thick hair. Her nose ignored the traces of sulfur in the air to savor the delicious smell of Joshua's skin. And her body barely felt the solid earth beneath the sleeping bag because it was so enthralled by the strength of his hard thighs pushing against hers.

All the while Beth was lost in her sensual discoveries, Joshua's fingers continued their careful preparations. They moved from stroking her shoulders to caressing her breasts again. "See how they swell into my hands; look how the tips have hardened to my touch," he murmured.

Calloused palms moved around the dark areas. Beth moaned and pushed hard against the strength of his hands, bidding him to knead her breasts, while she felt an ache begin to grow much deeper in her body.

"Living silk," Joshua breathed, moving over her stomach with fingers and mouth and tongue.

The wanting built in Beth when his hands coaxed her legs apart and touched the innermost softness of her skin. "I have to have you, Beth. There's nothing else I can do," he whispered almost in anguish. But his fingers were easing her own fears and had caused sensations in her that had built to a delicious agony.

"Oh, love me, Joshua, and let me love you." She reached out for him.

"Not yet," he murmured. "Not yet." He continued his tender stroking until Beth moved against his warm hand, fully ready to explore the unknown with him.

"Joshua!" she implored, and this time he took her into his arms.

"Now touch me, sweetheart." He pulled her hands to his chest, and Beth wound her fingers in the dark hair that adorned the massive expanse. She rubbed her cheek along the hard little nubs of his flat nipples, tonguing and sucking them to tautness.

Her exploration traced his well-healed scar, and then continued down the midline of hair that ended in a soft, thick mat surrounding the shaft of his need, which burned hotter than her own flushed skin.

This time Beth was no longer afraid. She transferred all the love she felt for Joshua to her fingertips and lips, adoring him, until he pulled her fiercely into the circle of his arms.

"Now, Beth . . . now, you will become mine!" The hoarse demand melted her with its sweet desperation.

Laying her tenderly back, his knees gently moved her legs apart, and then Joshua's massive body completely covered her slender form.

She felt her skin flush when the magnitude of his desire touched the citadel of her femininity. Ready to plunge into the sweet terror of the unknown realm, Beth joyously led Joshua to the portal of that ultimate closeness of body and spirit she knew destiny had meant them to achieve.

Sighing deeply, Beth wrapped her long, coltish legs around his hips, and then relinquished control to Joshua, trusting him to guide her. From his first slow, careful surge into her body, she knew that he had not been lying to her; he would bring her to throbbing fulfillment.

Although he was so very big, he had prepared her so well, there was no pain. Instead, each deep thrust he made sent a wave of sensual perfection throughout her shaking form.

As her body accepted his, Joshua tossed his head back and forth. She was so small, so tight, and yet she took him in, surrounding him completely with a clinging moist heat that threatened to make him forget anything he had ever known about restraint. But he ruthlessly denied a quick release to his own long-denied needs.

Joshua continued to give and give and give to her, designing each twisting movement of his bunching hips solely for her increasing pleasure. When Beth's small sounds of delight grew louder, he only increased his effort.

No longer having any fears about her ultimate destination, Beth began her own rhythm against his body, one of undulating feminine muscles that matched the pulse at his throat. As the sensual beat quickened, he groaned, slipping one large hand under her hips to bring Beth even closer and he plunged even deeper.

But then, just short of their mutual explosion, he exercised incredible control to stop all movement between them. He whispered desperately, "Tell me that you trust me. Say that you believe I'll keep you safe and never let anything harm you. Beth, you've got to say it . . . please!" he pleaded brokenly.

Beth pulled his head to hers, capturing his mouth in a deep kiss that sent emanations of pleasure down to the point of their joining. Of course she trusted him. She loved and worshipped him.

Beginning in a whisper, Beth reassured her demigod, "I do trust you, my love, with all my heart, with my very life!" she cried out.

Her words galvanized Joshua. Feeling as if an electric charge was running up his spine, he moved against her again. The hoarse moans of love that Beth uttered made him inexorably quicken his pace.

Beth was wracked by sensations she had waited for all her life. She was caught up in a blaze that threatened her with total extinction. As the wildfire reached its zenith, she gasped out an inarticulate utterance of release.

With Joshua's triumphant shout of confirmation in her ear, fierce pleasure raged through her body. She knew that the flare of her completion had set off an ecstatic eruption of consuming flames within him.

"Joshua, oh, how I love you!" she cried out while the world receded and she whipped her head back and forth against the huge hand that cupped it. Her nails bit deeply into the skin of his back as pleasure continued to surge through her body, fueled by the explosive release of Joshua's passion.

Pressing her burning cheek against the warm steel of his shoulder, she tried to hold on to the moment and her consciousness amid the overwhelming sensations.

An eternity later, Beth was finally able to lift her head, feeling the force of darkened eyes on her. She languidly smiled into those deep, changeable pools, only to be rocked out of her bliss by the pain evidenced there.

The purr that had been in her throat escaped as an agonized cry. Her hands flew to his face to caress the deep line between his eyes. She desperately tried to erase the grimace on Joshua's tightly clenched mouth.

"Joshua?" His name was the sum of her hurt and confusion.

His eyes fused shut; a bead of sweat ran down his cheek in an imitation of the grief she felt rise up in her. Because she loved him, Beth reached out to touch that tear of perspiration. She pulled her fingers back, feeling as if she had encountered acid when he called out in anguish, "Oh, my God, she's really gone!"

"Joshua, what's happening?" Her question was a whisper, but he heard and his accusing eyes snapped open.

"We've made her leave forever!"

Those words, and his sob, echoed around the tent. Joshua's full weight crushed down on Beth and he buried his face between her breasts.

ELEVEN

Self-hate and disgust rampaged through Joshua's body, but the shuddering of his own body couldn't dampen his awareness of how Beth was trembling beneath him. *Damnit, I've hurt her, used her,* he raged to himself, again realizing that he was cursed to injure everyone he cared for.

A half hour ago, when he had awakened from a nightmare, he had found golden eyes searching his, instead of deep blue. After that, the nominal battle he had waged against his desire for Beth had been a mockery. Joshua had willingly propelled himself into the final infidelity to a haunting memory.

Then Beth's sweet innocence totally captured his soul and he had pushed aside guilt. For a few wonderful minutes, he had forgotten culpability and surrendered his body to the most beautifully erotic experience of his life.

She had been incredible. Her small, eager form had completely accepted the demands of his suppressed desires.

Somehow, this soft little being had erupted into a seething flame that put to shame anything that volcano outside

179

would ever achieve. He had burned in her glory, skyrocketing to a plateau of feeling and sensuality he had never known before.

And when it was over, her ecstatic radiance had prompted his renewed guilt, his bitter self-anger. Beth's incandescent, gamine features had pushed out the memory of more classic planes and curves.

The smiling blue eyes and blond hair of his past would never come back to haunt his soul. Irrationally, he had put part of the blame for that on Beth. He condemned her for being the puzzle-piece that completed his life and for holding his tenuous grip on the future in the palm of her small hand.

Out of the feral animal's instinct for survival, he had unconsciously said the words that transferred some of the guilt away from his own overloaded brain. By so doing, Joshua had saved himself from going completely mad under that burden.

In some dim way, he understood the necessity for his actions, but how could he explain them to Beth. He couldn't tell her how much he felt for her; he didn't deserve to feel those overwhelming emotions again. He didn't deserve the sweetness of her body and the purity of her soul.

He had given up his right to happiness years ago when his true nature had been revealed as selfish, cowardly, impotent.

And now, history threatened to repeat itself. But this time he wasn't going to abandon the woman he loved. With self-loathing molding his features, Joshua mentally prepared himself to do what was necessary to get Beth safely off Mount St. Helens.

Long seconds had been stretched into an intolerable forever when Joshua finally raised his head.

"Get dressed," he commanded. "Let's get the hell away from this goddamn mountain."

Beth recoiled in horror at the look of total disgust flaring out of Joshua's tear-filled eyes. Trying to get away from his condemnation, she pushed at his shoulder. Joshua immediately rolled away, letting Beth escape from the suddenly degrading position beneath him.

Blindly, by instinct alone, she pulled on her clothes. Just as she finished, a flash of red on the floor snared her attention. Reaching for it, she discovered the material was Joshua's discarded briefs. Beth balled them up and threw them at his prone form with such force that she almost lost her balance.

Putting her hand down on the floor of the tent to recover her equilibrium, Beth's fingers encountered another object resting where the shorts had lain.

Lying next to Joshua's backpack, a small music box made out of carved wood had somehow rolled onto the floor. She focused her attention on it, not wanting to deal with the man lying facedown on the open sleeping bag, his fingers caressing the place where her head had been so recently.

She looked at the exquisite designs cut into the wood, obviously carved by an Oriental hand. The motifs of tree and mountain had the stylized perfection so treasured in that part of the world. With fingers still shaking in rage, Beth carefully rotated the box. Its construction was a marvel of the integration of form, line, and purpose.

Her fingers automatically wound the key to the playing mechanism. Just as she was about to open the lid, a subtle shifting of air currents made Beth aware that Joshua had gotten up and was standing next to her, his disturbing form still unclothed. He held his arms out to her in supplication, but appalled by his abrupt swings of behavior, she ignored the plea, glaring at him instead.

Then he saw what she was holding. She expected rage

because she had dared to touch something of his. Instead, he just accepted the wooden container when she held it out to him. Without a word, he slipped it into his backpack.

Turning away from him, not being able to bear watching him dress, Beth grabbed her own backpack and then went outside to tend to her morning needs. Afterward, she broke out the rest of the meager food supply and divided it for breakfast. Beth gave Joshua the greater portion his body would require—and then bitterly wondered at her concern.

There was an awful lump in her throat, but she forced herself to swallow a high-energy bar. Her body would need the fuel for this morning's hike. Beth had just choked down the last mouthful when Joshua came out of the tent.

He was fully dressed, his backpack already strapped to his shoulders.

"We'll be down to the clearing in less than two hours."

How could his deep voice sound so normal? she wondered as he continued speaking.

"I'm going to leave the tent and sleeping bag here. There's no need for you to weigh yourself down with anything more than a water canteen, and, of course, your cosmetic bag."

When Beth didn't respond to his feeble attempt at humor, Joshua went on. "When we get to Vancouver, we'll find out what happened to the rest of our personal belongings. In any case, I expect everybody will be spending at least one night in Portland."

Beth still didn't say anything, so Joshua knelt in front of her. She refused to look him in the eye and she cringed away from his touch.

"Please forgive me for what happened this morning. I lost control. Beth, we don't have any time now. But even if we did, I couldn't explain what happened here just now, or what happened here more than a decade ago . . ."

"Oh, you don't have to explain anything to me," Beth said, finally finding enough strength to unclog her throat.

"I understand completely." Who was she kidding? She understood nothing! She'd never be able to piece together what had changed the most overwhelmingly sweet experience of her life into a nightmare from which she would never be free. "Let's get out of here. I'd rather not get fried in your 'event.' " Her words were said coolly, in a dead, defeated voice.

In fact, an impending eruption no longer frightened her. She had spent so much emotion in the last hour that she didn't think any feelings would bother her very soon. There was only a subtle undertow of shame that she would have to avoid in the future when she recalled that look of contempt on Joshua's face after he finished making love . . . no, when he was done having sex with her.

Then the ground shuddered beneath them, effectively ending any further explanations or recriminations. Beth quickly found her canteen and catch-all bag, attaching them to her belt. "Are we going or not," she demanded.

"Beth, we're going. But, sweetheart, don't worry, we're not in danger of running into a pyroclastic flow here . . . even if any escapes the crater. Nothing is going to harm you. Not you, too." He shook his fist in the direction of the mountain.

Beth was completely bewildered. She couldn't understand the source of this new anger. Then she suddenly wondered if Vietnam had claimed the sanity of another veteran. No! She forced down hysterical giggles; it wasn't Vietnam—it was *her*. Beth Cristie literally drove the men in her life crazy!

Watching the strange expressions flit across Beth's face, Joshua suppressed the urge to pick her up in his arms. Instead, he took his goggles from his pocket and putting them on, effectively blocked out the mixture of pain and regret he knew was mirrored there.

Expecting it, he didn't react when Beth pushed away

his offered hand. He just turned down the trail, after making sure that she was going to follow him.

It took a mile, but beyond that, Beth had to concede that she had been wrong about her dulled emotions. Besides a barely controlled fury, creeping tendrils of fear wrapped her body as the restless earth increased its activity with each step they covered. Fighting down paralyzing panic, she only flinched when pebbles rolled by, seemingly of their own volition. However, she couldn't control her scream when five dead tree trunks appeared to dance along beside them for a dozen crazy cakewalk steps.

Yet, no matter how tempting it was to run, Joshua forced her to keep a trudging pace behind his broad body until they had reached a point still about a mile from the rendezvous site.

It was there that the volcano released its pent-up energy. The explosion was proceeded by tremors that grew to such an intensity, Beth fell to her hands and knees, unable to regain her feet.

The vibrations in the earth under her were augmented by a deep, rumbling sound from the mountain that filled her ears with pulsing waves until she was deaf to any other sound. It was instinct alone that made her eyes turn down the trail to see Joshua struggling to get back to her. His eyes were wild, his mouth was a wide-open slash. Beth finally realized that he was shouting at her and pointing at something behind her.

Twisting her head around, at first she didn't see what had frightened Joshua so much. Then, lifting her eyes higher, she finally focused on the dusty fall of loose rocks that had broken off the mountain's slope and was now surging down an erosion gully toward her.

It wasn't fire that would kill her, it was an avalanche. Unable to move, Beth could only stare while certain death approached. But when the bouncing stones were only a yard from her, Joshua's strong hands wrenched at her waist, pulling her toward him.

With bigger and bigger rocks cascading around them from every side, a bright-blue cone of light suddenly shimmered in the air. It seemed to Beth that the aura somehow repulsed the largest boulders, giving them the seconds needed for Joshua to push Beth to the ground behind a great stone monolith and cover her with his own tense body.

At first, Beth struggled against him. Then she felt the sting of wayward pebbles on her face and heard the sharp retorts from the crater repeatedly thundering overhead. She found herself clinging to his strong neck, her head buried in the comfort of his shoulder.

"I love you, I love you," she repeated again and again, confident that he couldn't hear her; horrified when she comprehended that it was still true.

Amid all the conflicting sensations, Beth could feel Joshua's lips moving in her hair, but she had no idea of what he was saying.

After several minutes, Beth felt the oppressive heaviness in the air lift a bit, and under her splayed fingertips, Joshua's muscles relaxed. His instinctive judgment proved correct. And as more seconds passed, Beth sent up a prayer of thanks that they were not going to be incinerated in a hot cloud of steam or crushed by flying boulders.

Hard sinew tensed again, and in one lithe movement, Joshua scooped Beth up off the ground. He whirled her around in the spontaneous dance of celebration.

"We're all right, sweetheart. My calculations were right on! It was just a minor event, like I said it would be. There's nothing more to worry about now. Beth, darlin', we're alive!" He planted a kiss on her nose, tightened his arms around her and then slid his mouth down to her lips, transferring his joy of survival into passion.

Beth held on to his body as the only solid object in the

still-rocking world. His heated kiss burned her soft mouth more than the suddenly tropic, acrid air whipping round them.

Just as his aroused body had done this morning, Joshua's masculine power surged against her tightly clasped form. When she felt the hard pulsation pressing into her, Beth couldn't help the instantaneous thrill that shot through her.

But just as quickly, anger and fear chilled her delight in being alive, negating her natural response to his nearness. She fought out of his embrace, beating at his arms and chest.

"Let go of me. Don't touch me again. You made it very clear this morning what you think of me—nothing! Well, the thought of you touching me again makes me sick!" she screamed at him. The force of her feelings carried her intent better than her hoarse, scratchy voice.

"Beth . . . Beth, my dearest love. I understand why you're angry with me, but all that really matters is that we're still alive, and I didn't lose you to this bitch of a mountain."

Beth quickly backed away when he reached a trembling hand for her.

"You were right in your predictions all along, weren't you, Dr. Hunter? There was never any real danger from this volcano, was there? The only menace was *you*, you crazy bastard!"

"Beth!"

Agony. So much pain was expressed in the single syllable of her name that Beth finally understood he was experiencing a torment equal to her own. With his hair whipping around his head until it formed a dark halo, Joshua looked like an anguished angel caught in a hot wind from hell.

"Oh, God, Beth." His husky words battled the turbulence to reach her. "Did I survive that avalanche only to lose you? Darling, I've just existed for so long. But since meeting you, I want to live again. Please say you'll stay with me, that you'll marry me.''

Suppressing a shudder that threatened to shake her apart, Beth forcefully denied the wild elation his proposal zipped through her body. She told herself that this was just another manifestation of his quixotic behavior. Marry him? After what had happened this morning when they finished making love?

Yet even remembering that shameful experience, she still had to fuse her lips together, sealing in the reply her heart wanted to give. *You've got to use your head*, she sternly told herself, *because this man has definitely lost his*. His reactions since this morning could have been part of a classic schizophrenic nightmare.

Easily reading Beth's thoughts as if they were marching across her forehead, Joshua's mouth curled around a sardonic self-appraisal. "Just neurotic, honey, not crazy." He chuckled wryly, but then his face sobered.

Beth froze when one long finger traced a gentle line along her lower lip and a calloused palm caressed her dirty, tear-streaked cheek. However, when his mouth descended toward hers, she took an abrupt step backward.

"No!"

With anguish twisting his face, Joshua pulled himself upright, acknowledging the panic in her refusal.

"Sweetheart, don't you know how much I love you?"

That declaration almost defeated her, but Beth refused to be seduced by this latest mood.

"That's too bad, because I'd be a fool to love you. How can you talk about love, about marriage?" she yelled. "How dare you? Don't you remember what happened this morning?"

"You're damn right, I remember. You told me you loved me . . . you showed me how much you loved me. I've never experienced anything like it in my life! As for what happened later, oh, hell, Beth, how can I explain?

I'll lose you if I do. Why can't we just think of our future and forget about the past?''

"No!" she shouted him down. "No," she then repeated softly. "Joshua, we have no future. No matter what I said or did, this morning was no more than a response to instinct, the snatching at life in the face of imminent death. Those events have no reality now. They're encapsulated in some parallel universe and have nothing to do with us. It didn't happen—forget it!''

Joshua vehemently shook his head, trying to think of some way to convince Beth of his feelings. "My God, sweetheart, maybe you don't know how special it was, because you have nothing to compare it to. Believe me, that depth of feeling is so very rare. I know that I've never felt it before.''

Instead of reassuring her, his words had sent flames of jealousy tearing through Beth. She might have nothing to compare this morning to, but on what did Joshua base *his* evaluation? On how many women? "Well, I guess I'll have to bow to your vast knowledge of the subject," she returned bitterly.

Joshua's soft answer cut through her anger with its understated ring of sincerity. "No, Beth, there haven't been many women at all. And none for more years than you'd ever believe. Even if the experience this morning wasn't as earth-shattering to you as it was for me, we have to think about the baby.''

"Baby?" she whispered.

"The child that might be forming inside you right now. We have to consider that eventuality. I don't want to wait for confirmation. If we get married right away, the license and the birth certificate will be dated a full nine months apart." He smiled down on her, hoping that would be reason enough to convince her.

Beth felt her knees unlock and she sank to the ash-covered ground; it was as if Joshua's words had actually knocked her off her feet.

"No. It isn't possible," she choked, the flow of her chaotic thoughts freezing with that denial.

"Oh, yes, darling, yes, it is."

"Well, don't worry about pregnancy. It's entirely the wrong time of month. I'm a biologist—I should know! Anyway, I wouldn't marry you for such a reason. I'd never tie anyone down like that."

Joshua knelt in front of her, putting his hands on either side of her face, not allowing Beth to move out of the gentle vise of his fingers.

"Then marry me because I need you, Beth. I need you more than Phillip Price does, and I love you more than he ever did. I don't care if he's a sick man and I'm playing dirty. *I* could never leave you in danger like he did. I won't give up like he did, either. You'll marry me, sooner or later, because we love each other. That's the simple truth of the matter, darling."

As he spoke, a thrill of twanging vibration raced through Beth. Although she instantly recognized that the physical sensation had been caused by a minor aftershock from the subsiding volcanic event, she knew that the emotional impact on her heart was the result of Joshua's insistence that they loved each other. Yet, what chance did they have? What future was possible for them when he refused to open up to her; when his past was such a mystery to her?

But why was he so afraid to reveal the cause of his pain to her? Sitting in the volcanic dust, Beth tried to organize the bits and pieces she had learned about Joshua Hunter in the last three days. It didn't take a genius to figure out that the overriding tenor of all their tension-filled encounters was that he *was* suffering—deeply.

He'd already told her that his misery wasn't caused by his experiences in Vietnam, so it had to be that a great love had gone wrong for him. A woman had abandoned him in some way, leaving him angered and in agony.

Only that could account for the behavior he was exhibiting. Beth intuitively felt that Joshua was being pulled apart by a force out of time. A mysterious feminine spectre from his past was destroying his present and blighting any future they might have had together.

Joshua's hands began caressing her face. Beth abruptly refocused on his features. The tension she saw there made her own hurting seem insignificant. He was examining her face with such an intensity that one might think his life depended on the decision she was trying to reach.

Seeing that desperation, Beth had to tell him the truth. "Oh, Joshua, I do love you." The words were said slowly, reluctantly. "But I can't marry you, unless I know what you're keeping from me. You have to tell me what's made you so angry, so hurt. You have to tell me about *her*."

She had said it so softly that at first it didn't seem Joshua had heard. Then he sank down next to her in the ash, shoulders slumped, head bowed.

"God, who told you about Carol? My dad? Ruth? No, they wouldn't do that. Woman's intuition, right? I knew it would come to this in the end. So, I'm damned if I do and damned if I don't," he said huskily.

His head lifted and Beth looked into the eyes of a dead man. For all his size and strength, he appeared so vulnerable and helpless that the acid of biting tears attacked her eyes.

Nevertheless she whispered, "I have to know."

He nodded and sat up straight. Flexing his wide shoulders, he shrugged out of the backpack he had been carrying all this time. He fumbled as he opened it, spilling the contents out at her feet.

Beth first noticed a man's wallet and then the exquisite little music box she had examined earlier this morning.

Looking up at Joshua, her eyes wide, Beth was immensely reassured when he just picked it up and placed it in her lap.

"This is part of the story . . . the last part. But I have to start at the beginning." He retrieved the wallet and took out a photograph.

Even as he handed it to her, Beth could see that Joshua's fingers were shaking. She wanted to thrust it back at him without looking, because she was sure that one glimpse at the picture would shatter her. When she finally regained her courage, Beth lowered her eyes to the photograph and found out that she was right.

A beautiful blond and blue-eyed young woman smiled out from the small square. The photographer—and it had to be Joshua—had captured an aura of vitality surrounding the girl. Then a bolt of déjà vu speared through Beth. The features, the eyes, the hair—everything—looked so familiar. Oh, there was a certain similarity to her sisters, but that was not it.

Several seconds passed while Beth tried to capture the elusive memory of where she had seen this face before. She finally tore her gaze away from the girl's golden features to look at the neat words penned in the lower, right-hand corner of the picture:

"To my husband, Joshua, the most important part
of my life, Carol"

This was Beth's worst nightmare. All her life she had come in second best to tall, blond girls in the love stakes. *Here* was Joshua's "type." For all his declarations of love, Beth was once again an also-ran.

"You said that you weren't married!" The accusation burst out of her, but her voice was no more than a sick murmur.

"Beth, she's been dead for almost twelve years." His

voice was tense and afraid. "I've tried so hard to tell you about Carol, but I couldn't. Because when you hear how she died, you're going to hate me."

Joshua reached over, and after putting the music box on top of his backpack, he lifted Beth onto his lap. Burying his lips on her neck, just below her ear, he chanted softly, "I love you. I love you, Beth. I love you so much, and now I'm going to lose you."

Two large tears squeezed out of her eyes, but they were tears of relief and joy. Somehow, his admission had touched something vital in her mind, in her heart. No matter whom he had loved in the past, Joshua loved her now!

"You won't ever lose me," she avowed, pulling away a little to look into his stricken eyes. "I don't care what you tell me. I won't let you go now. There will never be anyone else for me. There never was. Joshua, I was never going to marry Phillip. That was a fantasy in his mind. I just went out with him a few times. I'll never love anyone but you."

The words were hardly out of her mouth before Joshua sealed his lips to hers, capturing her promise between their heated flesh. Beth responded instantly, communicating her feelings to him by the soft little moans that were torn from her throat.

When he finally broke away, Joshua held Beth's head between his hands and saw the love in her eyes. He knew then that he could confess everything to her. For the first time, he was certain he could entrust their future to her understanding and forgiving heart.

"I should have told you about Carol on the night we met. But I didn't know you then. I thought I just wanted you. That was extraordinary in itself because until the other night in your tent, I hadn't wanted to make love to anyone since she died. She died here, Beth, when Mount St. Helens erupted back in 1980. This is where I killed her. This is where I murdered my wife."

TWELVE

Joshua held his breath, fearing that Beth would break away from him in horror.

A deep, involuntary sigh shook her body, but then she just put a soft hand on his cheek. "No, tell me what really happened," she said softly.

At her words, Joshua squeezed his eyes shut. And when he opened them again after long seconds, Beth realized that he was not seeing her, but was focusing on a painful event in his past. His next words confirmed her feeling.

"I . . . I met Carol at the army hospital in Honolulu while I was recovering from my wounds. I got one in the lung, just before my tour was over."

Remembering the long scar on his side, Beth had to restrain herself from unbuttoning Joshua's shirt and stroking that old wound. Instead, she forced herself to remain still, not daring to interrupt him now that he was lost in the past.

"Carol was a nurse," he was saying, "a lieutenant, who wasn't supposed to associate with a lowly noncom on a personal level. But she . . . she was kind and friendly, and I took advantage of those qualities. I told her all about myself, the horror of the war, my estrangement from Dad, and about my aborted education. As I got better, she encouraged me to reapply for college. Even though I wanted to marry her then, Carol kept things very cool so that I would actually leave when I was accepted at MIT."

"We hardly saw each other for the next five years. While she finished her tour of duty, I did my undergraduate studies in mechanical engineering. But we got married right after I graduated and her service was completed.

"We discussed where to go on our honeymoon. Carol suggested somewhere romantic—like Hawaii, a place where we could start a family. She was a few years older than I, and she wanted . . . Oh, God, Beth, she wanted a child so badly."

His voice had become so rough and raw that Beth tried to tell him to stop—that his pain was more than she could bear. But then he rushed on, obviously wanting to get it over and done with.

"Just before we left on our trip, Mount St. Helens started rumbling. As a joke, I suggested changing our plans and coming here for a volcano watch. Carol agreed immediately. She seemed to love the idea. She said that she had joined the Army in part because she wanted to see the world. Her face reminded me so much of how my mother used to look when she talked about visiting faraway places.

"So I rented a camper and we came up here for a month's honeymoon. I got so involved with exploring the area, so caught up with what the mountain was doing, that I kept extending and extending our time here. Even after the officials made us pull back out of what they thought was the danger zone, I didn't want to leave."

Abruptly, sliding Beth off his lap, Joshua got up and began pacing in front of her. Beth slowly rose and then put out her arms to him. The gesture stopped him, but not letting her touch him, he stood with fists clenched, looking fiercely at Beth.

"Didn't you hear what I just said? Because I was fascinated with this place, we stayed until it was too late. Beth, she's buried somewhere under the mud and muck that flowed into the Toutle River. We were within a few feet of safety when the bridge we were driving over gave way.

"Carol was tossed into the water, just as a wall of boiling mud and debris surged down on us. The front wheels of the camper locked into the twisted metal of a section of the bridge that eventually came to rest in against the shore. I was rescued a few hours later, but we never found any trace of Carol. Her body has never been recovered."

Joshua turned away, looking to the northwest, almost as if he could see the spot where Carol had died on the other side of the mountain.

"I killed her, Beth. She's dead because of me. I survived and did nothing to save her. Now, how can you possibly love a man who could do that!"

Trying to absorb some of his agony, while she sought to sift the gold of truth from the dross of his guilt, Beth grabbed for his shoulders and turned him back toward her.

"No! I know that's not how it happened," she insisted. "I've seen your courage during these last three days. You've protected me, putting your own body between me and danger over and over again! I'm as positive as I've ever been of anything that you didn't just *let* her die. First of all, why did she fall out of the camper while you didn't? Was she wearing a seat belt?"

A wretched silence lengthened between them until Beth squeezed his hand and prompted, "Joshua, was she wearing a seat belt?"

"No . . . she wasn't even in her seat. She was in the back of the camper."

"Why was she back there when you were racing away from the volcano?"

"Because she insisted on taking pictures. She was braced in the doorway, snapping photos of the cloud venting over the mountain. She was actually laughing, telling me to slow down so the camera wouldn't bounce so much. I yelled at her to get back into her seat and strap in, but she wouldn't listen. Then the bridge snapped. Just like that. Something must have hit me in the head, because the next thing I remember, I was upside down, hanging by my seat belt, almost roasted by the hot mud that was swirling by."

The large hands that grasped Beth's tightened almost unbearably, but she didn't react to the pain. It was nothing compared to what was reflected in Joshua's face as he finished his story.

"Carol was gone, vanished. I knew she was dead. I wanted to be dead, too. I tried to release the belt, but I couldn't reach it. A few hours later, a Forest Service helicopter rescued me, although I was unconscious by that time. They told me all about it later, in the hospital.

"I was in there for weeks, treated for burns and dehydration. When I was released, Dad took over as my nurse. He sat on me, kept me from killing myself. He shoved food down my throat when I tried to starve myself to death. After a while, I stopped trying to die, but I wasn't really living, either.

"For months I just sat in a chair, staring out the window. I wouldn't react to anything anyone said or did. Not to Dad or to the minister he brought to talk to me, or to the psychiatrist he dragged in.

"Dad finally got so mad at me, he threatened to throw me out on the next garbage day." Joshua chuckled ruefully, remembering his shock at the time.

"I said to go on, that's where I belonged, in a garbage dump. I was useless, as bad as he had been at keeping his wife safe.

"Well, instead of throwing me out, I thought for a minute that he was going to kill me and put me out of my misery. Instead, he said we should both do something to keep other men's wives from dying. We could prevent other people from being killed by Mount St. Helens or any other unpredictable mountain."

"But there's no way to stop a volcano," Beth couldn't help saying.

"No, but Dad suggested that we figure out a foolproof method to predict when one was going to blow and warn people away before it did. His suggestion saved my sanity. From that moment on, I dedicated myself to doing just that. I went back to school to learn about geology and got my doctorate in the subject. Over the last several years, I've worked on developing the equipment that could test my theories, that would prove the validity of my formula. I've studied active volcanos all over the world. And I finally got enough courage to come back here for the last trials before publishing our results."

"Then you have nothing to blame yourself for, Joshua," Beth broke in. "There was no way you could have saved Carol. She wanted those pictures; it was her decision to leave her seat."

"It was my fascination with the mountain that kept us here. We were supposed to leave days before the eruption on May eighteenth. We should have been back in our apartment by then, back in the city."

"People can die anywhere. There are no absolutes or guarantees in life," Beth disputed. "I'll bet the freeways Carol drove on every day were statistically a thousand times more dangerous than being near a volcano. And you know it, Joshua Jeremiah Hunter!"

"No . . . no," he whispered, "I killed her. It was all my fault."

He stood with his head lowered in shame, not about to admit that she was right. Feeling as frustrated as Stuart Hunter must have with Joshua's stubbornness, Beth searched her brain for some argument that would get to him.

A sudden and very dangerous idea formed in her brain.

"Well, Joshua. I guess I understand now. I know why you still feel guilty about Carol after all these years."

Beth waited a dramatic moment until Joshua finally raised his head to look at her. When he did, her next words were slow and measured for maximum effect. "If things happened as you say they did, there can only be one reason for your continued guilt. You really did murder your wife."

Joshua's mouth opened and closed, but his shock was so great he wasn't able to make a sound. Rushing on before he could recover, Beth continued her wild accusation.

"Yes, you must have planned your wife's death. Maybe it was all those army survivor's benefits you wanted. In any event, you somehow convinced Carol to get out of her seat to take the pictures. You probably told her that they would bring lots of money if you sold them to the newspapers. Then you guided the camper over the roughest part of the road. You must have known that the bridge was about to collapse and the wheels would catch so that you would be safe while Carol fell . . ."

Beth stopped abruptly, afraid she had gone too far when she saw a red tide of blood sweep up Joshua's neck and wash over his face.

"Cold-blooded murder? You think . . . Oh, my God!" As suddenly as it had come, the hot flush of color washed out of Joshua's skin.

Beth automatically reached out toward him, fearing that

her strategy had backfired. As if the earth itself was reacting to the agony in Joshua's eyes, the ground beneath
them rolled in a strong aftershock.

Flinging Beth's hand off his arm, Joshua swung away
from her and began striding down toward the pick-up site.

"You may think you're safer on your own," he threw
over his shoulder, "but I'm getting the hell off this mountain, whether you come with me or not."

"Joshua!" Beth wailed.

His long legs had put fifteen yards between them when
he abruptly whirled and stalked back to her. He grabbed
her by the shoulders and gave them two strong shakes.

"No, I'm not going to leave you. I told you that I'm
not like Phillip Price. I love you too much to abandon
you. But Jesus, Beth, how could you say that you care
for me and believe something so awful?"

"Oh, Joshua . . . I don't . . ."

"I didn't plan Carol's death!" his stronger voice bellowed over hers. "I would have gladly sold my soul to
the devil and died in her place. But since I didn't have
any occult powers, there was nothing I could do. Nothing
anyone could have done. Nothing . . . nobody . . ."

He sputtered to a ragged stop, his intelligence finally
catching up with his rage. A wretched sob and a gush of
scalding tears distorted his handsome features into a mask
of suffering.

"No, darling, there was nothing anyone could have
done in those circumstances." Beth softly finished his
sentence for him and wrapped her arms around his waist.

Holding tightly to his shuddering body, she soothed,
"Of course, I know you didn't really plan Carol's death.
I just wanted to shock you enough so that you'd finally
admit it to yourself. But . . . but you must have known,
subconsciously at least, that you weren't to blame for the
accident all along!"

In a flash of insight that was almost actinic, Beth rushed

ahead with the startling idea. "So there was something else you were *really* guilty about," she challenged, knowing that she was right.

Joshua was shaking his head, but he wasn't denying her words. When he finally spoke, his voice was husky with tears.

"I knew that you were a smart cookie, Beth. A lot smarter than me, it seems," he whispered. "You're right. I've known the real reason for my guilt, almost since the day Carol died. Yet I only let it surface when I met you. And then it hit me like a freight train. There you were, all tangled up in that damned experiment. I was so mad I was sputtering, but when I looked into your beautiful eyes, I knew instantly that I was going to fall in love with you. And somewhere between the time you linked me to Bozo the Clown and when I was patching up your elbows, I did fall in love." Joshua smiled at the look on Beth's face.

Then he sobered and went on. "At the same time, I finally acknowledged that whatever I had felt for my wife, it hadn't been love. So I had to deal with the guilt that realization generated the only way I could—I blew up at you. Then to add to the torture I was going through about Carol, I had to watch you with Price, thinking that I'd lost any chance of a future with you through my own stupidity."

"Oh, Joshua, I should have told you that I felt the same way about you from the first. I shouldn't have let you go on thinking that I might be serious about Phil," she moaned.

"You weren't to blame. I guess nobody was. Finding the right person is so hard. It's a rare, beautiful thing when the loving is equal. You and I are very lucky; Phil and Carol weren't."

It seemed to Beth that in finally facing his guilt, Joshua was ready to put it in perspective. Carol's death was in the past, and though he might think of her with pain and regret, it wouldn't be with the paralyzing guilt that had been tainting the present and destroying his future.

Two large hands tenderly stroked the tears off her cheeks. "Come on, Beth," he urged, "we've got to get going. That helicopter's supposed to be here soon. We wouldn't want to spend another night on this mountain, would we, sweetheart?"

As he talked, he quickly looked for his backpack, and then noticed the little box he had put down on it sometime during their emotion-filled discussion.

His face went gray under his tan.

"Oh, Beth. Carol's music box. I forgot about her music box. Before we came up here for our honeymoon, she made me promise that if she died before me, I would make sure to bury it with her. It was almost as if she had a premonition. But even though it was her wish, for years after her death, I couldn't even *look* at the box. I just put it in back of a deep closet. To this day, I've never been able to open it. When Dad and I planned this trip, I finally dug it out and brought the thing along to fulfill her request to bury it with her. But Beth, when I got here, I realized that I don't know where she is!"

Hearing the anguish, the fury, in Joshua's voice, Beth stumbled a step backward. She feared that his pain was going to make him lose control again.

However, he was shaking his head. "No, I'm not going to lash out at you, darling. I'll never do that again. This morning was the last time I'll ever take out my anger on you." His beautiful, changeable eyes probed hers. "Can I tell you what happened after we made love? Can we clear the air and put the past behind us?"

She nodded, though she was really ambivalent about discussing the bittersweet hour they had spent together.

"This morning, after we shared a taste of heaven, after I poured my love into you, the only thing I could think of was that I had robbed Carol. That was my real guilt, Beth. All I had ever given *her* was affection and desire.''

Joshua looked down at his clenched hands and then finally raised his eyes to Beth's. "I cared for her, but I just took from Carol. My needs, my wants, were always first. I gave her nothing, absolutely nothing. She wanted a family and I suggested that we postpone a bit. She wanted a real home and we had a dinky apartment. But worse than that, she deserved to be loved, and . . . and I should have set her free to find it with someone else. Well, I didn't, and now she'll never experience *anything,* again, save death—forever and ever.''

"Oh, darling," Beth murmured. Sharing his agony, she put her head on Joshua's chest, listening to the strong beat of his life force.

His deep voice rumbled on. "So when you looked into my eyes, after we made love, what you saw was not my anger with you, but at myself. When I yelled at you, I was trying to relieve myself of some of that rage. Can you ever forgive me for the pain I caused you today?''

Beth sighed, finally understanding the horrible episode.

"Joshua, let's forget the hurt we've done to each other. All I want to recall is the joy you gave me." Beth captured Joshua's broad shoulders between her hands. "Just remember, darling, that you don't have the patent on feeling guilty about an inequitable relationship. Whether or not it was true, Phillip *thought* he was in love with me. My rejection must have caused him a great deal of pain. And, Joshua, I didn't tell you everything about my relationship with my family . . .''

"Ruth mentioned something about your parents and sisters, Beth."

"She did? When did she—"

"The other night, when she read me the riot act. She

threatened to injure my . . . ah, more sensitive body parts, if I ever hurt you like your family had.''

"Well, I guess we both had to come to terms with the past. I'll have to make sure that Phil is getting the help he's needed all these years. You're going to have to let Carol rest in peace. I'm certain that she would want you to be happy, so don't ruin her final gift to you.''

At her words, Joshua again looked at the music box in his hand. As if his fingers had become numb, the little treasure tumbled from his fingers. Beth lunged for it, just as she had done the first day they met, when she saved something precious of his. Although she captured the box in her hands before it hit the ground, the catch holding the top closed somehow came undone. Its contents spilled out as the mechanism began a tingling version of the theme from "Carousel.''

As the music continued, Beth scrambled to pick up three items that had tumbled to the ash-covered earth. The first was a small photo of Carol in a wedding gown, standing next to a man in a military uniform. Even though she looked at it intently, it was several seconds before Beth saw that Joshua was not the man in the picture.

She turned it over, and on the back read the inscription in Carol's distinctive hand. "To Karl, the love of my life, on the happiest day of my life.''

"Joshua . . . Joshua," Beth whispered urgently. "Look at this.'' She held out the snapshot until he finally took it from her hand.

"I d-don't understand,'' he said after examining it carefully.

"Maybe this will explain more,'' Beth offered, showing him the other paper and the gold ring she had picked up.

The heavy folded sheet was a letter addressed to Carol Kramer. It was from Marine Lieutenant Karl Kramer's commanding officer. The text documented the courageous death of her husband in 1970. Karl Kramer had been awarded a posthumous Medal of Honor, along with the gratitude of his country.

"Carol had been married before," Joshua said, absolutely stunned. "He died three years before I met her, and she never told me."

"Perhaps it was because she couldn't, Joshua. Perhaps it was because it was too painful for her . . . just like you couldn't tell me, darling."

"But I was her husband!" Then he laughed harshly. "Her second husband. All this time I've felt so badly about not loving her like she loved me . . . and *he* was the love of her life."

"Oh, Joshua . . ." Beth began, not knowing how to soothe his hurt.

"I've had such horrible nightmares, Beth. Terrible dreams in which Carol came to me looking so sad . . . so blue . . . surrounded by blue. Like that flash of blue light during the avalanche."

"You saw it, too? My God, Joshua! *That's* where I saw Carol before . . . in my dreams. I had a dream about her the other night in your camp." Beth looked at the photo again. "Yes, it was Carol. She did look unhappy, and I had the feeling that she was trying to warn me about something. Then there were those pictures I took of you in the helicopter up in the crater."

Beth quickly told him about the blue halo of light that had appeared around him . . . but not Roger Mulheny.

"Joshua," she whispered, "she was here. Protecting you . . . protecting both of us in that rockslide. She does want you to be happy, to go on with your life."

As one, they looked up the mountain, to the slope they had rushed down so precipitously a short while ago.

It might have been a trick of light. It might have been a mirage reflecting off Spirit Lake, but they both saw a woman standing up there in a haze of blue. At her side was a man, his arm slung possessively around her shoulder.

As the music box ended its last repetition and the faint sound of the rescue helicopter reached their ears, Beth and Joshua saw the misty couple on the mountain slope raise their hands in farewell and fade into the shimmering air.

THIRTEEN

The sun had just set below the Los Angeles basin when the newlyweds returned to Beth's apartment. Parking the car, Joshua yawned prodigiously.

"Well, I don't know about you, wife, but I could sleep for a week." At the look on her face he drawled, "Eventually, my love, eventually."

When they got into the apartment, Joshua kicked the door shut with triumphant élan. Beth was sleepily nuzzling his neck, still holding on tightly after the traditional threshold crossing.

Staggering dramatically, Joshua made it to the couch, before he collapsed on to it, the slight burden of his bride on his lap.

At first, they just laughed with hysterical tiredness. Then they began recalling the events of the double wedding they had shared.

"I guess Dad and Ruth will be landing in Hawaii soon," Joshua began. "Boy, I don't know how we managed to get through the last few days. Packing up and closing down my place in Austin. Getting my seminar started at UCLA and then helping you arrange the wedding

206

on such short notice. It was enough to kill a man." He laughed, but then abruptly turned serious. "Beth, are you sure that you don't mind waiting six weeks for our own honeymoon?"

"Oh, Joshua. I knew that you had a commitment to teach the summer class. It wouldn't have been fair to the students if the university had to get a second-best substitute. Darling, I can wait for the honeymoon, I couldn't wait for you."

She aimed a quick kiss at his cheek, then closed in on his mouth. There, she found the sweet nectar that fed her rising hunger.

With that appetizer, fingers regained the energy to move in tender traceries, until exhaustion was only a memory and desire ran rampant between them. When she could stand it no longer, Beth slid off his lap and insistently led Joshua to the bedroom and the huge bed that had been delivered yesterday.

Standing next to it, Joshua quickly disposed of Beth's wedding finery, kissing and caressing each exposed area in turn. Beth decided it was only fair that she do the same for him.

Unbuttoning his shirt, she caressed the strong, prominent collarbones on each side of his thick-columned neck and then devoured the hollow where a heavy pulse thudded beneath her lips.

Her mouth slid down to his wide chest and moved along the soft covering of dark hair which tickled her nose as her tongue traced around his flat male nipples.

Joshua couldn't contain the groan that came hoarsely from deep in his chest. He barely controlled himself while Beth worked at opening his belt. Her lack of progress made him frantic. He desperately brushed her hands away to rid himself of his trousers and shorts.

When his glory was finally revealed to her, Beth immediately ran her hand down his absolutely flat stomach, straight to where the hair became heavier and the potent beauty of his manhood awaited her.

Well before fingers were done exploring, Joshua muttered ferociously. Picking Beth up, he rolled with a single, fluid motion onto the firm mattress and on top of her soft body.

Overwhelmed by this display of urgency, Beth was appalled when perverse laughter threatened to bubble out of her throat. She desperately tried to stifle it, but she lost the battle and a husky melody of giggles broke loose.

Joshua glared down at her. "What's so funny, young lady?" he demanded of his bride.

In her best imitation of the Saturday sportscaster, she intoned, "Did you see that, folks? J.J. Hunter picked up the football and, tucking it under his arm, he ran the last twenty-five yards in a brilliant burst of speed. Evading a tackle, he rolled into the end zone, protecting the ball with all one hundred ninety pounds of his handsome, lean sinew." Beth squeaked when his eyes glittered dangerously.

"The football doesn't mind," she protested. "It loves the feel of Hunter's one ninety, really!"

His dimple deepened with devilish intent, "Well let's not play football anymore. I think I'd rather play the Jockey and the Stallion. Guess who gets to be the jockey." He rolled once more with Beth still locked in his arms until she was uppermost, mounted on the living saddle of his hips.

Joshua reached down and firmly guided her into melding contact with his hardened body. Beth moaned with desire when he settled her on to him. Then she buried her head on his chest, trying to hide the rush of blood that broadcasted her embarrassment.

Stroking her hair, smiling to himself in loving appreciation of her freshness and basic innocence, Joshua tenderly lifted her face to place light kisses on her cheeks.

"I love you. You excite me beyond reason," he confided, caressing her bare shoulders and back, stroking her rounded hips and slender thighs.

In spite of her mortification, Beth felt herself responding to his words and his hands. She began to rub her cheek against his. The rough stubble of new growth scratched her skin with small pinpricks of pleasure.

She finally lifted her eyes to look into his. The love and desire radiating out of them melted her reserve. She placed her hands on his shoulders so that she could look down on him. She then arched her body until her breasts were near his lips.

Joshua kissed each inviting mound in turn, taking the tips into his mouth and turning them into hardened jewels. Slipping his hand between their fused bodies, he found the moist center of her desire and rubbed that love-swollen bud until Beth writhed against him.

Her movements became wanton as his body rose and fell to the tempo of the storm that began to claim them. Before the final wave could crash around them, Joshua uttered a wild cry. Rolling her over once more on the wide bed, he called her name.

Beth felt the first wave of incomparable pleasure tear through her body. The storm became a gale and the gale a hurricane. Each succeeding thrust multiplied the sensations until they were both tossed by a passion that scattered consciousness at its shattering conclusion.

Not quite sure when her mind returned, Beth eventually became aware of being gently rocked in the harboring cradle of strong arms and of being held securely against a vast expanse of chest. Joshua was kissing her and murmuring how much he loved her.

She took a deep breath and pulled his head down to her breast. With loving fingers, she stroked his thick hair and kissed the back of his neck.

"I can see why people get married. It makes all the

difference." She laughed raggedly and a shudder ran through the both of them at the memory of what they had just experienced. "But now that I know what joy is possible between a man and a woman, I don't understand how you could have *not* made love for such a long time."

Joshua sat up, but only to pull the covers over them. He settled back against the pillows with Beth held tightly to him before answering her question. They had vowed to be completely honest with each other, and he told her the absolute truth about his years of abstinence.

"First of all, Beth, it isn't like this for everyone. We are blessed in what we share. Many people just achieve a sort of release . . . a sense of peace. That's what I had with Carol. And after she died, I was too involved with my guilt to even notice my body's needs for a long, long time. When they finally resurfaced, I looked around and saw a lot of women. Very nice, very intelligent, very pretty women—and some of them were interested in me. Yet, how could I get involved with someone, when I couldn't offer anything more than that ephemeral escape from tension? It wouldn't have been fair. So, Beth, I . . . sublimated a lot with my work, and when my hormones ran too high, I took care of the tensions . . . by myself."

Joshua looked down at Beth. She wouldn't raise her eyes to his, but the heat of her cheek burning his shoulder told him a whole lot. "Hey, lady. My celibacy isn't any more bizarre than the case of a fantastic woman like you remaining a virgin till she was just shy of thirty."

Beth did look up at that statement and then smiled sweetly. "Maybe I was psychic, darling. Maybe I just had this picture in my head of a tall, handsome geologist who would make love to me like no other man ever could. I guess I didn't want to waste my energy on anyone who was just second best."

"I'll be forever grateful that you were so lazy," Joshua said, dropping one last kiss on her perfect little nose.

"Let's get a bit of sleep, sweetheart. Then tomorrow morning, you can make us our first meal as husband and wife."

"I always knew you were a closet chauvinist," she teased.

"No, I just plan to use a whole lot of calories in the morning, before we get out of bed. I imagine I'll be too wasted to do much more than grin after that," he muttered in a sleepy reply.

"In that case, I'm all for a certain division of labor," she said, bussing the rise of his bare shoulder.

Listening to his breathing even out, Beth smiled into the darkness. They had come a long way to reach this point. Carol's memory had clouded their first days together. Phillip Price had been another barrier they had to surmount. But Joshua had finally absolved himself of the tragic ending of his first marriage and she had relieved her own guilt about Phillip.

That troubled man had made a good start toward recovery in the last six weeks. Beth and Joshua had visited Phil at the Los Angeles veterans hospital soon after returning from Mount St. Helens.

There had been some tense moments, but then they had all been able to discuss what happened on the mountain with healing understanding. Now Phil was working again and seeing Dana Clark and had finally come to understand that it wasn't "unmanly" to ask for the help he needed to recover from the hell he had lived through in Vietnam.

With her eyes closing on that comforting thought, Beth snuggled closer to her husband's warm, strong body and slid into a contented sleep.

Sitting over a late brunch, Joshua stirred his freshly brewed coffee absently, and then put a warm hand over Beth's.

"It's time we thought about planning our future, sweetheart."

"OK," she agreed. "I think we should do the practical, everyday things most newlyweds do. First, a honeymoon in Manaus. You know, moon over the Amazon. Then we should enlist in the astronaut corps and be the first married couple on the moon. You'll be in heaven with the lunar rocks, and I'll look for evidence of an ancient alien invasion. But even if I can't find any strange life forms, just imagine the trip there and back: weightlessness on the journey, and one-sixth gravity while we're on the moon. Think of the variations!"

"You are shameless," Joshua laughed, pulling Beth onto his lap. "I had more exotic plans in mind. I didn't want to say anything until it was official, but the head of the geology department talked to me yesterday. They're offering me a full professorship. So, if you want, we can stay here, instead of going back to Texas. You shouldn't have to give up an opportunity like the one you've got at *Science in America*."

"Oh, Joshua!" was all Beth could say. The thought of having to quit her job before it really began had been at the back of her mind since returning from Washington State.

"OK. Los Angeles, it is." Joshua grinned. "Then I think we should be really reckless. Let's buy a house and have two or three kids in the next couple of years. That'll really be an adventure, don't you think?"

Beth looked into his eyes. Hers became warm and serious and shining. "That sounds like a good plan for the short haul. We can always go looking for Bug-eyed Monsters later, when the kids are out of kindergarten."

EPILOGUE

Beth dropped a quick kiss on the top of her brother-in-law's fiery hair after she changed his diaper. She gave his bottom a gentle push that sent him toddling over to his mother, who had just put pajamas on his equally red-headed twin brother.

Ruth groaned. "It'll be at least another year before these two poppets are out of diapers. I think I'll have Stuart buy stock in disposables. I'm just glad that we brought such a large supply with us. I haven't seen the kind I use any-where in downtown Mexico City." She suddenly laughed. "Listen to me. Listen to the Ph.D. in mass communications discussing nappies like it was the most scintillating subject in the world."

Bending, Ruth gave each of her one-year-olds a hug and kiss in preparation for their naps. She looked up at Beth. "You know, honey, it probably is. At least to this over-the-hill mother," she confided. "They'll always be a miracle to me. And as for Stuart, well, I don't have to remind you how proud he was to be a father again at his age!"

Beth hooted. "You two can give Joshua and me lessons

213

on energy and running after children, Ruth. You have more patience with your kids than I'll ever manage with my daughter. You're so even-tempered and logical with the boys," Beth continued. "As much as I love her, at times I have to fight to keep from screeching at my little angel."

"Well, I don't know about the logical part. When you start using reason with a one-year-old, you're asking for trouble. I guess I'm so tickled with them, I don't see them as the wild little Indians they truly are. Dan, Evan . . . bless you for keeping your mother young."

She took each by the hand and walked them to the third bedroom of their large hotel suite. Three cribs had been set up there for the children.

Beth followed behind, checking that her own year-old Carol Elizabeth was still asleep and covered. Looking down on her beautiful face, Beth admitted to herself that she was extraordinarily chauvinistic about her daughter. And with good reason! Beth and Joshua were sure that there had never been such a lovely, intelligent child born. Of course, Ruth and Stuart felt the same about their two children.

Carol had arrived within a week of the twins. The simultaneous pregnancies of the new Hunter women had helped bond the two couples into a strong, supportive family.

After softly singing a song for each twin and giving them a bottle, Ruth and Beth returned to the living room.

"Are you sure you don't mind taking care of three kids, Ruth? We can still hire a baby-sitter, and then you and Stu can come along with us to the ruins," Beth suggested.

"I'm very sure, dear. You know all that heat and humidity would just frizz up my naturally curly hair." She patted her head, smiling. "You and Josh go and enjoy yourselves. Stu and I will sit here and admire his medal!"

Beth laughed. Her father-in-law was unexpectedly smitten with the large gold medals he and Joshua had received yesterday from the grateful Mexican government.

Their seismic devices had saved thousands of lives in the previous year's 8.5 earthquake, which had been centered in the suburbs of Mexico City.

The government had been farsighted when they contracted for the devices and placed them around the tremor-prone capital. The three-day-early warning, along with the courage to evacuate five hundred thousand people from substandard buildings, had changed a potential major tragedy into just a week of inconvenience for those displaced.

The entire Hunter family had been invited to the city for the presentation ceremony. Beth also thought that Joshua and his father should have received invitations to Sweden, for a Nobel Prize in Physics. In fact, she was laughingly restrained by her husband from phoning the committee and protesting that his name wasn't on this year's list.

Looking at her watch, Ruth observed, "I'll bet I know why the men aren't back from the university yet. Stuart's Texas Spanish may not be up to the complexity of his subject, and he's too stubborn to ask for an interpreter. He's probably still thumbing through his dictionary for just the right word." She chuckled.

"Well, we've got three hours before our plane leaves for Mérida. I'm sure they'll be back in plenty of time. You know how Joshua is about punctuality." Beth rolled her eyes to the heavens.

They had had some words on the matter in their two years of marriage, but had finally worked out a compromise: Joshua no longer harassed Beth when they were running late, and she tried her best to organize her busy schedule to be on time . . . most of the time.

A key in the door signaled the return of father and son. Beth gave Joshua a big kiss in exchange for his bear hug. She covertly glanced at him while he told Ruth about the morning's presentation of their work to the University of Mexico's geology department.

His magnificent physique belied his forty-two years. His hard-won maturity did nothing but enhance the rugged handsomeness of his lean face. The deep tension lines he had when Beth first met him were gone. It testified to the happiness of their time together and the profound love that had grown between them.

Beth was little altered, too. She happily glanced down at one of the benefits of breast feeding, but she hadn't magically added any inches to her height. However, she had no need to compare herself to her sisters anymore. Beth no longer thought that elegance only resided in women over five feet nine. She knew that her physical being entranced Joshua and that her *soul* had entrapped him.

Her husband broke into her thoughts. "The university's going to send a car for us at three, Beth. Are we all packed?"

"Yes, sir, *we* are all packed, and I didn't forget your socks this time," she teased.

"Well, let's have our lunch from room service. Then you two can kiss the kiddies goodbye and take off for some time alone with the mosquitoes, snakes, and ruins," Ruth jested. "Stuart, how did your talk go?"

Stretched out on the couch where he was resting, Stuart answered without opening his eyes. "Honey, I must have done something right. My mouth is all sore from using my 'Spanish muscles,' " he informed her.

"Dad did very well, I thought. The interpreter they had on hand only winced three or four times during that whole speech," Joshua said, straight-faced.

After a leisurely lunch, Beth awakened the children. She and Joshua played with them until it was time to go. Carol was used to staying with her grandparents, so there was a minimum of tears at the separation.

Their plane landed in Mérida at dusk and they spent the night in the city of a quarter million people that perched on the bulge of the Yucatán Peninsula.

Beth and Joshua enjoyed an interesting evening with the combined archeology-geology staff from the University of Mexico. They speculated on just what would be found in the morning when they reached the Balancanche Cave, east of the ruins of Chichen Itza.

News of the discovery of several new passages in the cave had reached the school when Joshua was making a courtesy call. Rumors of startling statuettes and friezes of great detail and clarity were circulated through the faculty. An impromptu expedition was organized to evaluate the find as quickly as possible before any possible contamination from mold or bacteria could destroy the art work on the newly revealed walls.

As a courtesy, Joshua and his very excited wife had been invited to go along. Beth had a good supply of fast film and her best camera with her. She was already composing an article in her head for the next issue of *Science in America*.

They reached the site at nine the next morning, but government red tape and scientific caution kept them from actually getting into the new areas that day. The group was assured that they would be allowed in as soon as everything was ready. They were all urged to visit the main ruins of Chichen Itza, five kilometers west, until the installations of lights and plastic sheeting could assure the best conditions for the study and safety of the treasures.

So Beth and Joshua climbed the richly carved pyramids, marveled at the circular astronomical observatory, El Caraco, and wandered among the walls of the Nunnery and the Court of the Thousand Columns. The mixture of Mayan, in the old part of the ruin, and Toltec, in the "newer" section, was a contrast of conquered and conqueror.

They were especially impressed with the various representations of Quetzalcoatl, the feathered serpent, priest-king, who was supposed to have come to the ancients out of the sky, with gifts of knowledge that included the growing of corn.

The expedition pitched tents in the clearings outside the cave that night. The merry talk around a campfire and the singing of old folk songs was a poignant reminder to Beth of her first meeting with Joshua.

Later, in their tent, the special ardor with which he made love to her eloquently illustrated that his thoughts were on those days as well.

The wonder of their marriage was demonstrated anew, for while the love they shared had grown deep and mature, the passion that had initiated it had not diminished. Indeed, their need for that particular aspect of love had increased, to make every consummation a renewal of their vows to each other.

When the fury of this night's events reached the conclusion of their ecstasy, Beth pulled Joshua's head down to bury his mouth against her breast while she burrowed her lips into the hollow of his neck. Thus, they were able to muffle the explosive sounds that issued from their throats as they reached their coruscating finale.

"I'm glad we're alone, darling," Joshua said when he could articulate again. "I still think that family togetherness is important, but it's so nice to be with you like this, little one." He kissed the moisture off Beth's forehead and zipped them into their double sleeping bag.

"It's heaven," Beth agreed. "This is far better than those field trips where the coeds outnumber the rugged professors, fifteen to one. And don't forget that I'm still going on every one with you!" Beth reiterated an old "discussion."

"How can I forget what you've brought up every three months since we were married? Beth, have I ever given you any cause to worry, honey?"

"No, you haven't. It's all those man-hungry girls I'm concerned about. So I'll remain eternally vigilant, you great big delicious hunk." Beth gave him a mock bite on the ear and snuggled into his arms, ready to sleep. Both of them had smiles on their lips as they drifted off.

All the preparations for the scientific appraisal of the new find were completed by nine-thirty the next morning. Beth checked out her equipment carefully, and followed behind Joshua and the others as they quickly went through the older portions of the cave. The group skirted the lake that was the home of blind fish and shrimp and passed through plastic sheeting barriers into the tunnels of the newly discovered section.

When they entered, they were amazed at the number of niches that had been cut out of the living rock. Almost every one contained an offertory urn highlighting reverence for the gods—chiefly those to the rain god, Tlaloc. Yet, as interesting as those were, what had really gotten the discoverers of this section so excited last week was the large frieze painted on the far wall.

The mural's colors were a brilliant combination of sulfur yellow, russet umber, and cerulean blue detailing. The subjects were done with the exquisite detail of the Toltec master craftsmen.

However, Beth and Joshua heard the scientists mumble to themselves that these artifacts were far older than the Toltec, or even the Mayan reign. Everybody stood in silent awe of the scenes which were so realistically portrayed.

Stretching from one end of the tunnel to the other were views of the great god Quetzalcoatl. The sequence of events traced his arrival among Man, the giving of gifts, and his teaching about the wonders of agriculture and science.

Beth had taken one look at this representation and moaned. She found herself leaning against Joshua's wide chest for support. He had gazed from her to the frieze and back again. The awe on his face turned to glee. He squeezed his wife to him and shared her elation at the sight.

For Beth, it was as if she were back on Mount St. Helens, where she and Joshua had poured out their life histories to each other and discussed the wonders of the universe.

She looked into her husband's laughter-filled eyes and felt again the loving and sharing of those first moments they had spent together. They had forged a relationship that had survived the crucible of a volcanic eruption and every other problem.

Turning back to the mural, Beth focused again on the detailed art work. The rendering of Quetzalcoatl was probably the earliest-known representation of the god. Unlike later images, this was *not* a man dressed in feathers and scales.

Instead, Beth saw a ten-foot-high illustration of a jaunty- and sophisticated-looking pocket dinosaur. Dressed in what certainly could have been a complicated space suit, it merrily gazed out at Beth, spanning the countless centuries with the force of its friendly personality and giving nature.

After communicating with that lifelike painting for endless minutes, Beth finally turned to pull Joshua into a fierce embrace and whispered into his ear.

"There is a season of love, and you, beloved, have made mine endless. But there is also a season of wonder. And I think that ours has just started."

No. 89 JUST ONE KISS by Carole Dean
Michael is Nikki's guardian angel and too handsome for his own good.

No. 90 HOLD BACK THE NIGHT by Sandra Steffen
Shane is a man with a mission and ready for anything . . . except Starr.

No. 91 FIRST MATE by Susan Macias
It only takes a minute for Mac to see that Amy isn't so little anymore.

No. 92 TO LOVE AGAIN by Dana Lynn Hites
Cord thought just one kiss would be enough. But Honey proved him wrong!

No. 93 NO LIMIT TO LOVE by Kate Freiman
Lisa was called the "little boss" and Bruiser didn't like it one bit!

No. 94 SPECIAL EFFECTS by Jo Leigh
Catlin wouldn't fall for any tricks from Luke, the master of illusion.

No. 95 PURE INSTINCT by Ellen Fletcher
She tried but Amie couldn't forget Buck's strong arms and teasing lips.

Meteor Publishing Corporation
Dept. 692, P. O. Box 41820, Philadelphia, PA 19101-9828

Please send the books I've indicated below. Check or money order (U.S. dollars only)—no cash, stamps or C.O.D.s (PA residents, add 6% sales tax). I am enclosing $2.95 plus 75¢ handling fee for *each* book ordered.

Total Amount Enclosed: $_____.

___ No. 65	___ No. 77	___ No. 84	___ No. 90
___ No. 82	___ No. 78	___ No. 85	___ No. 91
___ No. 96	___ No. 79	___ No. 86	___ No. 92
___ No. 74	___ No. 80	___ No. 87	___ No. 93
___ No. 75	___ No. 81	___ No. 88	___ No. 94
___ No. 76	___ No. 83	___ No. 89	___ No. 95

Please Print:
Name _____

Address _____ Apt. No. _____

City/State _____ Zip _____

Allow four to six weeks for delivery. Quantities limited.